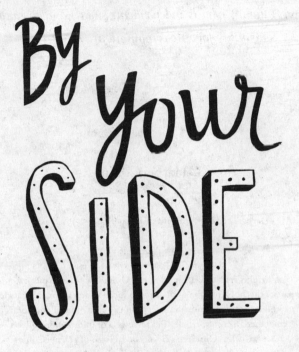

BY YOUR SIDE

KASIE WEST

HARPER TEEN

An Imprint of HarperCollinsPublishers

*To my Autumn, who is independent, smart, and so sarcastic—
one of my favorite combinations. I love you!*

HarperTeen is an imprint of HarperCollins Publishers.

Library of Congress Control Number: 2016949939
ISBN 978-0-06-245586-4

Typography by Torborg Davern
17 18 19 20 21   PC/LSCH   10 9 8 7 6 5 4 3 2 1
❖
First Edition

CHAPTER 1

• • • • • • •

I was locked in the library trying not to panic. Literally locked. As in, no escape. Every door, every window, every air vent. Okay, I hadn't tried the air vents, but I was seriously considering it. I wasn't desperate enough . . . yet. My friends would realize what had happened and they'd come back and free me, I assured myself. I just had to wait.

It all started when I had to go to the bathroom. Well, before that there had been a lot of soda—a two-liter of Dr Pepper that Morgan had smuggled into the library. I had drunk more than my fair share of the bottle when

Jeff sat down next to me, smelling like trees and sky and sunlight every time he leaned over to ask my opinion.

It wasn't until the windows darkened to black, the librarians asked us to leave, and we made it all the way to the underground parking garage where the fifteen of us were dividing into four cars that I realized I wasn't going to make it down the street, let alone all the way to the canyon campfire.

"I have to pee," I announced after I plopped my bag into Jeff's trunk. Lisa rolled down her window. Her car, parked next to Jeff's, was already running. "I thought you were coming in my car, Autumn." She gave me a knowing smile. She knew I wanted to go with Jeff.

I smiled too. "I'll be right back. There is no toilet at the bonfire."

"There are a lot of trees," Jeff said, rounding the car and slamming his trunk shut. It echoed through the nearly empty garage. In his car I could now see three heads in the backseat and a fourth in the passenger seat. No. They all beat me to it. I would have to go with Lisa after all. No big deal, I'd have plenty of time to talk to Jeff at the bonfire. It wasn't in my nature to be bold in my declarations of undying affection, but with my limbs all jittery from nearly two liters of caffeine and Lisa's warning about Avi stealing Jeff out from under me buzzing in my head, I felt powerful.

I rushed back down the long hall, up the stairs, and through the glass walkway that overlooked a courtyard. When I made it to the main floor of the library, half the lights were already out.

The library was too big and needed more bathrooms, I decided by the time I made it there. I pushed open the heavy wooden door and quickly found a stall. The box holding the paper seat covers was empty. Looked like I'd have to hover.

As I was zipping my pants back up, the lights went out. I let out a yelp then laughed. "Funny, guys." Dallin, Jeff's best friend, had no doubt found the breaker. It seemed like something he would do.

The lights remained out, though, and no laughing followed my scream. They must've been on motion detectors. I waved my hands. Nothing. I inched forward, feeling along the door, trying not to think about all the germs clinging to it, until I found the lock and slid it open. A streetlight shone through an upper window, so I was able to see just enough for a thorough hand washing. It was an eco-friendly bathroom, meaning only air dryers. I wiped my hands on my jeans, opting for speed over the most inefficient way ever to dry hands. My reflection in the mirror was only a shadow, but I leaned forward anyway to see if my makeup was smudged. From what I could tell, it looked fine.

Out in the hall only a few random overhead lights illuminated the way. The place was completely shut down. I picked up my pace. The library at night was creepier than I'd thought it could be. The ten-foot-long enclosed glass hallway sparkled as snow began to fall outside. I didn't linger like I was tempted to. Hopefully the snow wouldn't affect the bonfire. If it stayed light, it would make it magical. A perfect night for confessions. Jeff wasn't going to freak out when I told him, was he? No, he'd been flirting with me all night. He'd even picked the same era as I had for the history essay. I didn't think that was a coincidence.

As for the cabin with the girls after the bonfire, the snow would be perfect. Maybe we'd get snowed in. That had happened once before. At first it had stressed me out but it ended up the best weekend ever—hot chocolate and tubing and ghost stories.

I reached the door to the parking garage and gave the metal bar a shove. It didn't budge. I pushed a second time. Nothing. "Jeff! Dallin! You're not funny!" I pressed my nose against the glass, but as far as I could see both ways there were absolutely no cars or people. "Lisa?"

Out of habit, I reached for my cell phone. My hand met only the empty pocket of my jeans. I'd put my black weekend bag with all my stuff—cell phone, clothes, jacket, purse, snacks, camera, medication—in Jeff's trunk.

No.

I ran the entire library, searching for another way out. A way that apparently didn't exist. Six doors to the outside and they were all locked. And so there I was—back leaned up against the door to the parking garage, its cold seeping into my skin—stuck in a big empty library, caffeine and anxiety battling it out in my body.

A heart-fluttering panic worked its way up my chest and took my breath away. Calm down. They'll be back, I told myself. There had just been too many people getting into too many different cars. They all thought I was with someone else. Once the four cars reached the bonfire, someone would notice I wasn't there and they'd come back.

I calculated the time that would take. Thirty minutes up the canyon, thirty minutes back. I'd be here for an hour. Well, then they'd have to find someone with a key to open this door. But that wouldn't take much longer. They'd all have phones. They could call the fire department if they had to. Okay, now I was getting dramatic. No emergency departments would have to be called.

My pep talk helped. This was nothing to get worked up about.

I didn't want to leave my post for fear my friends wouldn't see me when they came back. Or I wouldn't see or hear them. But without my phone or my camera I had no way of passing the time. I started humming a song very badly, then laughed at my effort. Maybe I'd just count the holes in the ceiling panels or . . . I looked around and came up empty. How did people pass the time without cell phones?

". . . skies are blue. Birds fly over the rainbow." My singing wasn't going to earn me a record deal anytime soon, but that hadn't stopped me from belting out a few songs at the top of my lungs. I stopped, my throat raw. It had been at least an hour.

My butt was numb and the chill from the floor had crept up my body, making me shiver. They must turn the heat down on the weekend. I stood and stretched. Maybe this place had a phone somewhere. I hadn't thought to look until now. I'd never had to look for a phone. I always had my phone with me.

For the seventh time that night I walked back through the glass walkway. Everything was white now. The ground was covered in snow, the trees frosted with it. I wished I had my camera with me to capture the contrast of the scene—the dark lines of the building and trees against the stark whiteness of the snow. I didn't, so I kept walking.

I started in the entryway, but couldn't find a phone anywhere. There might have been one in the locked office, but a big desk blocked my view. Even if I could see one, I obviously didn't have a key. Past a set of double glass doors was where half the books lived. The other half were behind me in the children's section. It was darker in there, and I lingered by the doors for a while, taking in the space before me. Large, solid shelves filled the center, surrounded by tables and seating areas.

Computers.

Along the side wall were computers. I could send an email or a direct message.

It was even darker once I stepped all the way inside. Some table lamps were spread throughout the area and I reached under the shade of one to see if they were for decoration or if they actually worked. It clicked on with a warm glow. By the time I made it to the computers, I had turned on three lamps. They did little to dispel the darkness in such a large space, but they created a nice ambience. I laughed at myself. An ambience for what? A dance party? A candlelit dinner for one?

I sat down in front of a computer and powered it on. The first screen that lit up in front of me was a prompt to enter the library employee username and password. I groaned. Luck was not on my side tonight at all.

I heard a creaking noise above me and looked up. I don't know what I thought I'd see, but there was nothing but darkness. The building was old and probably just settling in for the night. Or maybe it was the snow or wind hitting an upper window.

Another noise from above had me walking quickly to the hall. I jogged up the stairs and reached the front door. I pulled on the handles as hard as I could. The doors stayed firmly closed. I looked through the narrow side window. Cars drove by on the main avenue in front, but the sidewalks were empty. No one would hear me if I pounded on the glass. I knew this. I'd tried earlier.

I was fine. There was no one in the library but me. Who else would be dumb enough to get trapped in a library? All by themselves. With no way out. Distraction. I needed a distraction. I had nothing with me, though.

Books! This place was full of books. I would grab a book, find a faraway corner, and read until someone found me. Some might've even considered this scenario a dream come true. I could consider it that too. There was power in thoughts. This was my dream come true.

CHAPTER 2

startled awake, and it took me several moments before I remembered where I was—trapped in a library. The book I had picked out to read rested open on my lap and my head had flopped onto the armrest of the chair. My neck screamed at me as I sat up. I rubbed at the knot there. A clock on the wall above the checkout desk read two fifteen.

Why wasn't anyone worried about me? Searching for me? Maybe they were. In the wrong places. Had they all thought I went to the bonfire? That I decided to go home from there?

My parents were going to kill me. It was never easy talking them into letting me spend the weekend up at the cabin with the girls. I'd had to negotiate hard. My mom was a lawyer and way too good at making me see things her way, so I always went to my dad first. Plus, he worked from home (*Creating the perfect tagline or jingle for your business.* His words, not mine.) so he was the one available to take requests. Once I had him on my side we could normally convince my mom together. The negotiation had gone something like this:

"Dad, can I go up to Lisa's cabin this weekend?"

He spun his desk chair around to face me. "Which one sounds better? 'Tommy's, because every day is a donut day.'"

"Ooh. Every day *is* a donut day. I haven't had mine today yet."

He held up his finger. "Or. 'Tommy's, they're hot and fresh.'"

"Who's hot and fresh? That sounds like you're talking about a house full of frat boys or something."

"You're right. I need the word *donuts* in there, don't I?" He spun back around in his chair and typed something in his computer.

"So? Can I go this weekend?"

"Go where?"

"Lisa's cabin."

"No."

I wrapped my arms around him and laid my head on his shoulder. "Please. Her parents will be there, and I've done it before."

"The whole weekend seems a bit long for you."

I gave him a smile while putting on my best pleading face. "I'll be fine. I promise. I won't go out at all next weekend. I'll stay in and help around the house."

I could tell he was softening, but I hadn't quite got him. "And I'll hang out with Owen next time he's in town."

"You *like* to hang out with your brother, Autumn."

I laughed. "Or do I?"

"Your mom's firm has a work dinner in a couple of weeks. If you can handle a weekend at a cabin, you should be able to handle that."

Nothing could have sounded worse to me. But that's what compromise was—giving up something for another thing you wanted more. "Okay."

"Okay," he said.

"I can go?"

"I'll have to double-check with your mom, but I'm sure it will be fine. Be safe. Take your phone. Your rules for the weekend: no drinking, no drugs, and call us every night."

I kissed his cheek. "Those first two might be hard, but

I can definitely handle the third."

"Funny," he said.

Call them every night. I hadn't called them tonight. I wouldn't call them tonight. That would put him in full dad mode. He'd call my friends. If they hadn't understood why I wasn't there before, they'd understand that somewhere along the way I'd gotten left behind. Someone would put two and two together. Sure, my parents would never let me leave the house after this again, but at least someone would find me.

My head ached, so I found my way to the drinking fountain outside the restroom. At least I had water. And nothing else. *Nothing* else. I shook my head. Those were the wrong thoughts. Someone was going to find me soon. If not tonight, then in the morning, when the library opened. I couldn't remember what time the library opened on Saturday mornings. Ten? Eight more hours. Easy.

It was getting colder in the building. I found a thermostat box on the wall, but it was locked. This place sure seemed overzealous about their security.

In the distance I could barely make out a steady beat. There was music coming from somewhere. I ran to the front door and saw a group of people walking by on the sidewalk, laughing. They held a phone or iPod or something that was glowing in the darkness and playing music loud enough for me to hear. I banged on the glass and yelled. Not one of them turned or paused. Not one of them looked around like they even heard the hint of a noise. I banged again and yelled louder. Nothing.

"Listening to music too loud damages your hearing," I said, resting my forehead against the glass. That's when I saw a white paper below me, taped to the window. I peeled it off and read the front. *The library will be closed starting Saturday, January 14, through Monday, January 16, in observance of Martin Luther King, Jr. Day.*

Closed for the *entire* weekend? All three days? I'd be stuck here for three more days? No. I couldn't do this. I couldn't be in a huge building alone for three days. This was my worst nightmare.

My heart was beating so fast now it felt like my chest was being squeezed. My lungs weren't expanding like they should. I yanked on the chains wrapped around the handles of the front door. Pulled them with all my might. "Let me out."

A voice in the back of my head told me to calm down before I made this worse. Everything was fine. So I was stuck alone in a library, but I was safe. I could read and jog the stairs and stay busy. There were plenty of distractions here.

In my new quiet state, I heard something behind me. Footsteps on wood.

I whirled around, pressing my back to the door. That's when I saw a shadowy figure on the stairs, a metal object glinting in his right hand. A knife. I wasn't alone after all. And I definitely wasn't safe.

CHAPTER 3

I stayed as flat against the wall as possible. Maybe the person wouldn't see me. No, that was unlikely, considering that seconds before I had been banging on the wall and pulling the chains on the door. I might as well have been screaming, *I'm trapped in a library all alone and am desperate to get out!*

What was my plan now? I could run somewhere. Lock myself in a room. Though as far as I knew all the rooms that had locks were already locking me out. Just when I was about to run somewhere, anywhere, to find a weapon or somewhere to hide, he spoke.

"I'm not going to hurt you. I didn't know anyone else was here." He held up his hands and then, as if just now realizing he held a knife in one, he bent down and tucked it into his boot.

That didn't make me feel much better. "What are you doing here?"

"Just needed a place to stay."

Great. I was trapped in the library with a homeless guy? A homeless guy with a knife. My heart was in my throat.

I could tell he was trying to talk in a calm voice, but it came out scratchy. "Let's sit somewhere and talk. I'm going to get my bag. I left it at the top of the stairs. And then I'm going to come down. Okay?" His hands were still raised in front of him, like that action should make me feel perfectly at ease. "Don't call anyone until we talk."

He thought I was going to call someone? If I had access to a phone, I wouldn't be here. If I had access to any communication device—a bullhorn, a Morse code machine—do those machines have names?—I wouldn't be here. But I wasn't going to give away my hand. "Okay," I said.

The second he left me alone, I ran back down the stairs and past the glass doors. If he was armed, I wanted to be too.

I tucked myself behind a shelf in the back stacks. My

breath was heavy and uneven and I couldn't see a thing. I reached in front of me and grabbed the biggest book I could find. Worst-case scenario, I could hit him over the head with it.

"Hello?" he said from across the room.

"Don't come any closer."

"Where are you?"

"It doesn't matter. You want to talk? Talk." If I acted tough, maybe he'd think I was.

His voice became louder, clearer, so he must've been walking toward me. "There's no reason to be scared of me."

Why couldn't he just stay across the room? We didn't have to be within spitting distance to talk.

As I went to take a step back, my knee hit the shelf and one book and then another slid to the ground with a thud. I tightened my grip on the book I held and took off for the door. He was faster, though, and cut me off. I held the book over my head.

"Stop," I said.

He took a step closer. I threw the book at him. He dodged it. I picked up another from a nearby shelf and threw it. It hit his shoulder.

He held his hands over his head. "Really?"

"I already called the cops," I said.

He cussed.

I threw another book. "So just leave me alone. They'll be here any second."

We were closer now, one of the lamps I'd turned on earlier glowing to our right. That's when I realized I recognized him.

I gasped. "Dax?"

"Do I know you?"

I must've still been in the shadows.

In relief, I lowered the book I held. Dax Miller wouldn't have been my first choice of guys I'd want to be locked in a library with. In fact, if I could choose any guy from my high school, he probably would've been the last. His reputation wasn't exactly stellar. There were stories about him. Lots of stories. But he wasn't a stranger. And I wasn't scared of him, so I immediately relaxed. "You go to my school."

I wasn't sure he knew me like most people at school did. I was on yearbook and was constantly snapping pictures so I was everywhere all the time. It was hard not to be well known when I had to be involved in so many events. But I'd never taken *his* picture. He wasn't involved in anything. Well, at least not anything school-sponsored.

I took a small step forward, into the soft glow of lamp-light, so he could see me more clearly.

Recognition crossed his face as he took me in, from

my shoulder-length light-brown hair to my black wedge boots, then back up to my eyes. He didn't seem to like what he saw. "Did you really call the cops?"

"No." I ran my hands over my pockets. "I don't have a phone."

His eyes skimmed over my pockets as if he didn't believe me, then he nodded once and headed toward the bag he'd dropped next to a chair.

I followed after him. "Do you?"

"Do I what?" He unzipped his bag.

"Have a phone."

"No, I don't."

I stared at his bag, not sure he was telling the truth. "I just need to call my parents. They're probably worried sick about me. Nobody knows where I am." At least that's what I was assuming since nobody had come back. "I would just use it to tell them where I am."

He pulled a sleeping bag from his duffel and spread it on the floor. "I don't have a phone."

He brought a sleeping bag to the library? He wasn't trapped here like me. He'd planned on staying all along? "But you're not homeless," I said.

"I never said I was."

"Why are you here?" I asked.

He crawled into his sleeping bag and then reached up and turned out the light.

"Why were you worried about me calling the cops anyway? Are you in some kind of trouble?"

"Can you keep it down? I'm trying to sleep."

If my whole body didn't feel like Jell-O I might've kicked him, but instead I stumbled to a chair, sat down, and put my head on my knees. This shouldn't have surprised me. Dax was secretive at school, a loner—why would I expect him to tell me his life story now?

It didn't matter. It was fine. I'd be fine. At least I'd established Dax wasn't trying to kill me or hurt me. Even though Dax was . . . well, Dax . . . it was better not being trapped here alone. And he had to have a phone in that big bag of his. He'd brought a sleeping bag, after all. When he went to sleep, I'd look through his stuff and find it. Now that I had a game plan I felt much better.

My chest slowly relaxed, relieving my burning lungs. This was the weirdest thing that had ever happened to me. It might even be a funny story later. Much later, when I was home with my parents and in my own bed with my nice warm comforter.

It was cold in here.

I stretched and then laid my head on the arm of the chair, pretending to go to sleep. I wasn't sure if he could see me or if he was even watching, but I wanted him to think I was sleeping. Then, when I was sure he was out, I'd find his phone, call home, and this would all be over.

The clock on the wall read 3:20. My eyes ached from being awake for so long. I wondered what my friends were doing. What Jeff was doing. I'd known Jeff since freshman year, liked him since junior year, and now, in my senior year, had decided it was now or never. We'd both be going away to school the following year, and before we left I'd wanted to see if the tension that hummed beneath the surface whenever he was around would translate into a good relationship.

Had it only been that morning when he'd stopped me in the hall at school? My mind replayed the exchange.

"Autumn!"

I turned, camera in hand, and snapped his picture. He was easy to photograph, his features soft, open, friendly. His smile lit up his whole face, made his green eyes sparkle and his olive skin glow.

He caught up with me. "You might have more pictures of me than my parents."

I probably did. "I can't help that the camera loves you."

"Is the camera asking me out on a date?"

"This camera goes nowhere without me."

He raised his eyebrows like he wanted me to follow through with what I was implying. I wanted to ask him out. So bad. But if I had to be the one doing the asking, it wasn't going to be in the middle of a crowded school hallway.

He went on. "So I was thinking about getting a group together to go to the library tonight and work on that history paper Mr. Garcia assigned. You in?"

I probably should've said no, but when offered extra time to hang out with Jeff, I always tried to make it work. "Yeah . . . I want to. I'll have to talk to Lisa. We're going up to the cabin with Morgan and Avi."

"Let's go before that, and then on your way up to the cabin we can stop at a campground and have a bonfire to celebrate finishing our papers."

I laughed and pushed lightly on his shoulder. "You have this all planned out."

"I do. So, you can work on the girls?"

"Yes. I'll make it happen."

"I knew you would. I'll ask Dallin and the guys. See you tonight."

And he saw me, before he left me locked in a library. If Jeff and I had been trapped here in this library instead of Dax and me . . . that would've been fun. He would've already figured out how to slide down the wooden stairs or race the book carts down the hall. Jeff was the exact opposite of Dax. Jeff smiled easily and joked often, and when he was around everyone was always laughing. Dax was dark and serious and seemed to weigh down any situation.

Jeff. Where was he? Had something bad happened?

Did he think I ditched out on him at the bonfire? Why didn't anyone realize I was gone? It didn't matter. Soon I'd have a way to let everyone know where I was. Soon I'd have a phone.

CHAPTER 4

• • • • • • •

The scene around me was hazy, blurry. The sensation was familiar, but my mind wouldn't clarify what was going on. I was in a cold room with no windows or doors. It was like a big icebox. The second I thought it, the walls became slick with ice, the floor as well. Everything was covered in ice. My teeth began to chatter so hard they hurt. And then a musky scent enveloped me. Like one of Jeff's hugs. And then Jeff was there, hugging me. The ice room disappeared, replaced by an endless green field. We stood in the middle clinging to each other.

"I liked you all along too," he whispered. "I don't

know why it took us so long to admit it."

"Because I was scared," I said.

"Of what?"

What was I scared of? Letting someone close? Handing him the power to hurt me? Letting go of control? Possibilities don't hurt as much as realities. Possibilities are exciting and endless. Realities are final. That had always held me back with Jeff, the thought that if I said how I felt and he didn't feel the same way back, that would be it. There would be no more "what ifs," no more "might bes," no more dreaming.

Dreaming. That's what this was. Just a dream. It was all just a dream. I needed to wake up now.

My eyes fluttered open. Sun shone through the upper windows, lighting the room. Disappointment weighed heavy on my chest. I may have been dreaming, but being trapped in the library hadn't been a dream. I was still here. Still stuck.

With Dax. He was no longer lying on the floor. Where had he gone?

I sat up quickly and saw spots, the sleeping bag slipping off my shoulders as I steadied myself. His sleeping bag. He'd put his sleeping bag on me. I let it fall all the way to the floor and then stared at it lying there useless. I immediately missed its warmth.

It was eight o'clock and my stomach was tight from

hunger. Nobody had come for me.

"Did the sleeping bag offend you?"

I let out a short scream. Dax sat in a chair across the room, his legs stretched out in front of him, crossed at the ankles. He wore jeans and a long-sleeved black shirt. His dark hair was slightly damp and was drying in a thick wave. He had a shadow of growth along his jaw. He held an open book, propped against his chest. The position he was sitting in—one shoulder down farther than the other, the shadows playing on his face creating shapes of darkness, the contrast of the red book against his black shirt . . . something made me wish I had my camera.

"You shouldn't sneak up on a girl like that."

"I didn't move."

"I know. It was a joke. I just didn't see you at first. Thanks . . . for the sleeping bag." A chill went through me, betraying the fact that I still needed it. "I . . . I have to go to the bathroom."

"No need for a running commentary."

"I was just telling you . . . right." I stood, pulled down my left pant leg that had somehow ridden up during the night, and went back to the restroom. The toilet seat was cold, and the mirror proved I was in worse shape than I'd thought. Mascara was smudged down both sides of my face, making my hazel eyes look darker than normal.

My hair, perfect waves the day before, was now a tangled mess, and three days without face wash was going to cause the world's worst breakout. I turned on the water and did my best job to clean up the stray mascara and rinse my mouth out with water.

I finger-combed my hair to acceptable. There was still a kink in my neck from the awkward angle at which I'd slept, and my stomach was not going to be happy with me if I didn't find food at some point today. I was angry with myself for falling asleep the night before instead of following through with the find-Dax's-phone plan. Why was he making this so difficult? Why did he care if people knew we were here, anyway? Was he in some sort of trouble with the law . . . again? What had he done this time? I wasn't even sure what he'd done the first time. Rumor had it that he'd beat up some guy. It wouldn't surprise me if that rumor had been true.

I shivered again. I had been so thrilled with my outfit last night—a teal-green, flowy T-shirt, a cute tailored jacket, and a pair of jeans. But it had been warm in the library when we were working. Hot, even. For the hundredth time I wished I hadn't taken my jacket off and shoved it in my bag. Wished I hadn't put my bag in Jeff's trunk. My bag. If I had *that* this whole thing would be over. Even without my phone I would've had everything I needed to last the weekend.

There had to be food in this place somewhere. The librarians had to eat lunch. A break room, maybe? On the third floor, I found it—a kitchen. There was not only a fridge but two vending machines—one for soda, one for snacks. They were kind of cruel really, the food on display without any way of getting it. I kicked the soda machine as I walked by, thought about reaching up and trying to grab one from the wide slot below, but quickly dismissed that thought. I'd once read a story online where a guy had to be rescued by the fire department because he got his arm stuck in a vending machine.

The fridge, unlike every other thing in the library, was not locked. It was a huge catering fridge. I'd almost forgotten that people had weddings and events at the library. It really was a big, gorgeous building that had become my prison. I crossed my fingers and opened one of the doors. On the shelf in the middle was the corner of a sheet cake. I wasn't even sure why anyone would save it—that's how small it was. But I would gratefully eat it later.

Behind the next silver fridge door was a clear Tupperware container of who-knew-what, but I could see the dark spots of mold clinging to the sides. Aside from that were two mystery paper bags. I pulled out the first bag with the words *DON'T EAT MY FOOD* written on the outside in Sharpie and looked inside—an apple and a yogurt, which was over a week expired. Considering the warning on the outside, I had hoped for something more steal-worthy. I took the apple and left the yogurt for later. In the other bag was more Tupperware and a can of soda. I gingerly lifted out the plastic bowl and slowly opened the lid. No mold, but I also couldn't tell what it was. Pasta? Vegetables? Smelling it didn't help. That could wait. I took the soda and left the rest.

In the cupboards I found some coffee cups and split the soda into two. The drawers were free of real utensils, but I found a plastic knife. It immediately broke when I tried to cut the apple in half with it. I'd just eat half and hope Dax wasn't a germophobe.

I washed the apple for thirty seconds under warm water, then took a bite. Nothing had ever tasted better. I found some napkins tucked away in a drawer, and when I had eaten my share, I wrapped up the remaining half, picked up the cups, and went back down the stairs to face Dax again. If I could just get him to trust me, I wouldn't need to sneak into his bag. He'd gladly hand over his phone to me. And he would. I was nice. People liked me. Dax would too.

CHAPTER 5

• • • • • • •

The main library was bright during the day; plenty of windows brought in slanting rays of sunshine. I carried the two mugs by their handles and held out one for him to take.

"You found coffee?"

"Coke close enough?"

He relieved me of one of the mugs and then I held out the apple wrapped in a napkin.

"What is it?" he asked without taking it.

"It's half an apple."

"You found half an apple?"

"I found a whole apple. I ate half of it. I can eat the whole thing if—"

He plucked it from my still outstretched hand.

"You're welcome."

He raised his glass to me and took a chug.

Not even a thank you. "One of the librarians must be an apple thief. The bag where I found it was owned by someone accustomed to having their food stolen. We have now added to the distrust."

"I'm sure you'll replace it later."

"Maybe I will." I made my way back to the chair I had slept in. His sleeping bag still sat on the floor. I stared at it for a long moment really not wanting to have to use it, but the goose bumps on my arms were multiplying by the second, so I swallowed my pride and picked it up. I draped the sleeping bag over my shoulders and sat down, holding my mug between two hands, wishing there was a hot drink inside.

Once this soda was gone we could share a yogurt and some cake later and maybe a mystery dish. I could practically feel my stomach shrinking. Unless . . .

I looked at the big bag by his feet.

When I glanced up, he was staring at me. "What do you have in there?" I asked.

He must've known exactly what I had been staring at because he answered, "Not much."

"Food? If you were planning to stay the whole weekend, you must've brought something to eat."

"I wasn't planning on staying here the whole weekend."

"Where were you planning to stay? Why did you end up here?"

"I was planning to stay somewhere else."

I waited for him to clarify, but that was the extent of his answer. "You're not a big talker."

"I talk when I have things to say."

"Was that supposed to be insightful?"

"It wasn't supposed to be anything but an answer."

This was going to be a long weekend.

He closed the book and placed it on the table next to him, then leaned forward, his elbows on his knees. "Why are you here?"

I wanted to give him a snarky answer to compete with his responses. Something like, *I wanted to eat stolen apples and read books all weekend.* But I held my tongue. Maybe if he learned more about me, he'd realize I just wanted to leave. I wasn't here to ruin whatever plan he'd had when coming here. "I had to pee."

He leaned back and picked up his book, as though I really had given him my fake answer.

"We were here, working on that history project Mr. Garcia assigned. Did you do that yet?"

He must've realized I was actually answering his question, because instead of opening his book he placed it in his lap and shook his head no.

"Anyway, we were here, a bunch of us, and we stayed past closing to finish our papers. Everyone was leaving, getting in cars, and then I had to pee."

"Your friends left you?" Now his expression changed. He was surprised.

"There were four cars. Lisa thought I was going with Jeff."

"Your boyfriend?"

"He's not my boyfriend . . . yet. But anyway, Jeff's car was full so he must've thought I went with Lisa or Dallin or someone. But I was with nobody . . . obviously."

"Obviously."

"Are you making fun of me?"

"No. I'm confused."

"About which part?" I set my now-empty mug on the table next to me.

"About the part where they didn't come back."

"Well, that's the part I'm confused about too." Sort of.

"Some sort of hazing?"

"You think my friends were hazing me?"

He shrugged. "So it was an *accident*? They all accidentally forgot about you?"

"They wouldn't do that. They must've thought I went

home or maybe they didn't realize this is the place they lost track of me and are looking for me somewhere else right now." I'd already gone over a million theories about why they hadn't come back for me, each one worse than the last. I'd had to stop before I drove myself crazy with worry.

He uncrossed his ankles and sat forward again. "Lost track of you?"

"I don't know where they are. I don't know why they didn't come back. There's a reason, and it's a good one, and we'll all laugh about it when I get out of here. We'll laugh, and it will all make sense, and it will be a story I'll tell forever. The time I got stuck in the library with the—"

I stopped abruptly. My cheeks went hot and I looked down at my shoes. I wasn't sure how I was going to finish that sentence but no option had been a good one. The criminal? The druggie? The druggie's son? I'd heard it all.

He raised his eyebrows. "Finish. You were doing so good."

"Sorry."

"Why?"

"Never mind. That's my story. What's yours?"

"Mine?"

"Why are you here?"

He held up his book. "I wanted to read."

"And eat stolen apples?"

"What?"

"Nothing. It's just, I told you why I was here, and that's what I get in return?"

"There aren't any books in my house. Well, unless you count the Good Book. But that's mainly used to condemn me." He ran a hand through his hair and didn't continue. Like he had said too much.

But he hadn't said anything. "Fine. You don't have to tell me. When we get out of here we'll go our separate ways."

He sighed. "Speaking of. I'm not sure how you're going to spin this when we eventually get discovered, but can we just tell our own stories? You go with the pee one, and I'll let myself out when the doors are opened and go my own way."

"I can't tell people you were here?"

"You can do whatever you want. Tell your friends you were stuck here with the . . . whatever . . . but the librarians, the cops . . ."

"What about the cops?" I asked, wrapping the sleeping bag tighter around my shoulders. "Why are they going to be involved?"

"If someone reported you missing, they will be involved."

"What if someone reported *you* missing?"

"They didn't."

"Why not? Don't you think your parents are worried about you?"

"No."

"Are you in some kind of trouble?"

"No. I'm not. But I don't want trouble."

"You won't get it from me." At least that's what I was saying now while I was trying to earn his trust. And his phone.

Hopefully his phone would be easier to get than his trust. Because I could tell his trust wasn't something he regularly granted.

CHAPTER 6

●　　●　　●　　●　　●　　●　　●

I'd heard lots of rumors about Dax the last two years. Lisa, who prided herself on knowing everything about everyone, had told me the most, in rushed whispers anytime we would see him around at school. He had transferred in the middle of sophomore year. His attendance was irregular. The beginning of junior year he'd spent a few months in juvie. When he came back he had a tattoo on the inside of his left wrist and was quieter than ever. He didn't have any friends as far as I could tell and I never saw him during lunch. Outside of school, I saw him even less. One time he was at the movies with some girl I'd never seen before. He'd never acknowledged my existence. Not that I cared. He was just another kid from school.

I could tell he didn't want to acknowledge me any more now than he had then by the way he looked at me. Did he even know my name? I realized he hadn't said it once. I wasn't sure how things would go down when we were finally discovered here, but it was in my best interest for now to tell him what he wanted to hear. "Nobody needs to know."

He went back to reading without a word of gratitude. Did he not know how to say thank you?

I reached down and unlaced my boots. I'd been wearing them too long and the tops of my feet hurt. I slipped them off, wondering if it was a good idea. I was only wearing a thin pair of ankle socks and my feet immediately became cold. I pulled them up onto the chair with me and tucked them under the sleeping bag.

"There were vending machines in the kitchen but I don't have any money . . . do you?"

He shifted in his seat, reached into his back pocket, and pulled out a wallet. He opened it and produced a single bill. I couldn't tell from where I sat if it was a dollar or twenty or something in between. "I take it all your belongings somehow ended up in one of those four cars that left without you and hasn't returned."

"They'll be back."

One corner of his mouth lifted into a smile. Oh good, I amused him. "That's all I have," he said, pointing to the table where he'd dropped the bill. "Spend it wisely."

"I'm not hungry right now, so we can wait."

"That half an apple filled you up?"

"We're on rations here. If we have to last until Tuesday, we need to space our few meals." A yogurt, the cake, the Tupperware bowl of mystery, and whatever the money would buy us, that's all we had for three days or until I could find his phone. He'd leave his bag unattended at some point.

"Twelve hours trapped in a library and you're already a survivalist."

I crossed my arms. "You seem to enjoy making fun of me."

"I was being sincere. I mean, if ever in a real life-or-death situation, you've already learned how to throw books and scavenge for food."

The books I had hurled at him the night before were in a messy pile behind him. I needed to clean those up. "Well, if you're ever in a life-or-death situation you can read and dole out insults."

"I'm reading about how to survive living with a spoiled rich girl for three days."

Spoiled rich girl? He didn't know me at all. Sure, my

parents had money but they were annoyingly good at making me work for things. "Considering you don't want me to tell anyone about you being here, you sure are good at making me want to do the exact opposite."

He let out a huff of air. "I can tell by the way you look at me that you're not going to keep your mouth shut. You've already figured me all out."

"You don't know anything about me."

"Everything I need to know is written all over your face."

"Right now the only thing my face should be conveying is that it thinks you're a jerk."

He bowed his head as if to say, *exactly*.

Ugh. I'd never met anyone more frustrating. I couldn't believe I still had three full days with him. I had to get out before then. I *would* get out before then. In the meantime, I didn't have to sit here and be insulted.

I made my way back to the glass hallway. The glass must've had some special coating on it, because it wasn't fogged up at all, nor was there snow sticking to any of it. But there was snow everywhere else. I was surprised by just how much. It came all the way up to the low windows I could see across the way. That was a lot of snow. Maybe this was why nobody was looking for me. Had everyone been snowed in at the cabin?

My bag was in Jeff's trunk. Didn't Jeff realize I hadn't

made it up when he saw that? Maybe he hadn't looked in his trunk. It was Saturday morning. He was probably still in bed. When he woke up and looked in his trunk . . . why would he look in his trunk? This was so messed up. My hope of being rescued before Tuesday when the librarians reappeared was dwindling with every passing minute.

I couldn't stand in this hallway much longer. It was freezing. I ran through and down to the door of the parking garage for another look. Nothing had changed. I was going to have to start doing laps in the library if it got much colder.

Not wanting to go back upstairs, I sat down in front of the door, imagining Jeff's car pulling up, him stepping out, smiling at me through the glass as though this was all part of some funny joke. Everything in life was funny to Jeff.

Like the day before, when I had been searching for a World War II book in the history aisle of the library and Jeff had come up behind me.

"I think I grabbed the book you were looking for by accident."

"By accident?"

"I heard you mention your topic; it must've stuck in my mind."

I smiled and reached for the book he was holding out.

He raised it just out of my reach. When I laughed he held it out for me again, only to do the same thing. I sighed and waited for him to place it in my hands this time, which he did.

"Do you think Mr. Garcia forced us to use the library for this assignment because he hates Google or because he's old school?" Jeff asked.

"Probably a little of both, plus he knew it would make it harder on us. I really think he wanted us to spend our whole weekend on this."

"We probably shouldn't have written 'history is a thing of the past' on the board. I think it set him off."

I laughed. "We? You wrote that on the board. I was going to write: 'history spelled backward is yrotsih.'"

Jeff tugged lightly on the ends of my hair. "That would've been funny. You should've."

I could never have done that. It had made me nervous enough watching him.

"Mine was a joke too. I think Mr. Garcia liked my super clever observation about the subject he teaches," Jeff said.

I laughed. "He does seem to like you."

His finger skimmed along the book next to my hand. "Everyone likes me, Autumn." He winked in my direction. He may have said it as a joke but it was true. Everyone did like Jeff.

"When's the last time you were in a library?" he asked.

"When I was a kid. My mom used to take me to the Mother Goose reading time they did here. That lady who dressed up like an old woman. I still have no idea why they called her Mother Goose. We should research that today. Forget World War II. This is the information we really need to know."

"So true. If they called her Mother Goose, she should've been dressed up like a goose, not an old woman. Let's find the librarian and ask her to enlighten us." Then he cupped his hands around his mouth. "Librarian!"

"Shhh," I hissed.

He laughed and whispered, "What? Did I do something wrong?"

I smiled. "Maybe we should actually read something so we can get our papers written and get out of here."

"Right. Homework. That's what we need to work on." He pulled out a book and flipped through the pages, but his gaze never left mine.

I dropped my eyes. Behind Jeff, about waist high, a head appeared to be sitting on a shelf, disembodied. I yelped before I registered it was Dallin. Jeff turned around.

"You both need to get ahead on your reading," Dallin said.

Jeff took the two books that Dallin's head was resting between and proceeded to use them like a vise, smashing his head.

"Don't crush my genius!" Dallin yelled.

"You're an idiot," Jeff said.

Dallin couldn't stop laughing long enough to back his body out of the shelf. I was sure we were seconds away from getting kicked out of the library.

"What are you doing?"

I gasped, pulled out of my memory by Dax's question. I shifted on the floor to look over my shoulder. "You seem to have a habit of sneaking up on people."

He was in the open doorway at the end of the hall, twenty feet away. "I called to you twice."

"Oh. Well, I was thinking." When he didn't respond I added, "Did you need something?"

"There's a TV in the break room. Thought you might want to know."

"Break room?"

"Yes."

"I didn't see a break room when I searched the library yesterday."

"I guess you missed it, then. The TV only gets local stations, though."

I pushed myself to standing when he walked away. It was nearly noon. I wasn't sure what played on local channels at this time, but I wasn't going to turn down television. I rounded the corner and jogged to catch up with him. "So, what? Soap operas?"

"It's Saturday."

Right. Not soap operas. Cartoons? Whatever it was, it was something. "You know the soap opera schedule well?"

"By heart," he said straight-faced.

Next to the door he approached was a small square electronic box. We'd need some sort of employee badge to open the door. Which we didn't have. Dax didn't seem to care about that; he jiggled the handle a little and gave a hard pull and it swung open. How often had he stayed at the library, anyway? He seemed to know this place well.

"How'd you do that?"

"It's an old building. Some doors are more pliable than others."

I followed him in. "Which doors?"

"None to the outside."

But what about other ones? Ones that might have phones in them? I'd have to try all the doors again later.

Dax stopped in front of a vending machine. He surveyed the items on display behind the glass. I went immediately to the fridge that I hadn't yet explored. I opened it and found nothing but old ketchup packets.

I closed it with a sigh and joined him by the vending machine.

I still had no idea how much money he had. Would we get one bag of pretzels or five? I thought maybe we'd take a vote on what to get, but he slid his bill in the slot and began pushing buttons.

"I don't have any food allergies," I said, my passive-aggressive way of telling him he wasn't being thoughtful.

"Good," was all he said back as a bag of chips dropped from its slot. He gave the machine a shake but nothing else jarred loose with the effort. On the digital screen it showed he had four dollars left. He pushed a couple more buttons and this time a Payday dropped. He repeated the shaking motion with the same result.

He retrieved his two items from the slot then stepped aside and gestured for me to make a selection. Oh. Had that been his plan all along? That we'd each get to pick a couple items?

"Thanks," I mumbled and stepped up to check out my choices. "I'll pay you back."

"No need to."

I settled on Cheez-Its and a Payday as well. I figured the peanuts were the closest thing in the machine to healthy and maybe filling. There was a dollar left, so I stepped aside.

"Any preference?" he asked, taking in the selection.

I shrugged. "Not really."

"Anything you absolutely hate?"

I raised my eyebrows at him and then smiled.

"In the machine," he said, not taking my bait.

"No, whatever you want."

He chose another Payday. Probably a good choice.

It was a small room, which I would think would mean it would be warmer than if it had been in the main part of the library. But it wasn't. It was probably because a window, fogged with frost, took up a big portion of the back wall.

Dax picked up the remote to a television that sat on a metal rolling cart. He handed it to me then left the room without a word.

Okay, guess he didn't want to watch television, just quarantine me. I must've completely ruined his weekend. His weekend of what? Reading? Being alone in a big library? Maybe he'd planned on stealing something here and I'd ruined that. Did the library have anything to steal?

I pointed the remote at the television and pushed power. I flipped through the channels—golf, tennis, cartoons, an old movie. I stopped there, sat on the couch, and opened the Payday.

"Was this the only choice?" Dax asked, coming back into the break room. He now had on a sweatshirt and was carrying the red sleeping bag, which he plopped on my lap before sitting down on the opposite end of the couch.

I was so surprised that I stuttered out, "N-no," and handed him the remote.

He changed it and stopped on the cartoon—*Scooby-Doo*. I wrapped myself up in the sleeping bag. It smelled good, musky, and I wondered if that's what Dax smelled like up close. Then I wondered why I would wonder something like that.

We watched the cartoon in silence for several minutes before I said, "You'd think after the thousandth time of the monster actually being a person in disguise that they'd check and see if he had a mask on *first*."

"Then it would be a two-minute show." A small smile played across his lips. Maybe he had a sense of humor in there somewhere after all. Buried deep. Maybe at the bottom of his duffel bag.

His bag. It was in the other room alone, unsupervised. He was just opening his candy, settling into the couch. He even put his feet up on the coffee table. I had at least ten minutes. I made a show of stretching. I had taken two bites of my candy bar. I needed to save it for later anyway. I tucked it back into its wrapper and set it on the table along with the Cheez-Its.

"I'll be right back. Bathroom."

"No need—"

"Right. You don't want to know." How hard was a simple *okay*? I was used to telling people where I was going because I was always with a group, not that it had done me much good last night. Maybe he wasn't used to having to report his whereabouts because he was always alone. I looked over my shoulder as I reached the door. His focus was entirely on the television. This was perfect.

CHAPTER 7

●   ●   ●   ●   ●   ●   ●

When I got to the library section, Dax's bag wasn't where I'd seen it last. Had he hidden it? But then I realized he'd just tucked it under the chair. I rushed forward, knowing I didn't have a lot of time, and squatted down. The black handle stuck out so I gave it a tug. It was wedged a little and it took me a couple of good yanks to free. I listened carefully to make sure I didn't hear him coming.

Undoing that zipper was the loudest five seconds of my life. It seemed to echo through the whole room as I held my breath. Once it was open I glanced over my shoulder to make sure I was still in the clear. I was. The bag contained everything an overnight bag might: toiletries (I was going to kill him for not telling me he had toothpaste), extra clothes, socks, a couple of protein bars (was he planning to share those?), and finally, finally, at the bottom of the bag I found what I was looking for. A phone. It was an old flip one and when I opened it the screen was dark.

I wasn't sure how to turn it on. I held down the side button for a few seconds. Nothing happened. So I tried the button with a picture of a green phone on it. Still nothing.

"Really?" Dax said from behind me.

I twirled toward him, still in my squatting position, and immediately lost my balance and fell on my butt. His phone was now held out in front of me in plain sight.

"You have a phone," I said. "I'm stuck here and you have a phone."

"You went through my things?" It was a question but the anger in his voice made it more of an accusation.

"I had to, because you told me you didn't have a phone, but you really do. I just want to call my family. I'm sure they're worried about me."

"Go ahead." He pointed to the phone.

Was this some sort of a trick? I looked at the black screen again. "I can't turn it on."

"Exactly." He plucked it from my hand, shoved it back into his bag, and zipped it up.

"What do you mean *exactly*? Can you turn it on for me?"

"No, I can't. It has no minutes and no charge."

"Oh." I still sat on the floor and was too deflated to get up. "Well, that's not very helpful."

"You know, before coming here, I forgot to think about you and your needs."

"Why would you pack a dead phone? Is the charger in there?"

"You tell me."

"Why did you follow me down here, anyway?"

"Because you left the room looking guilty, like you were about to commit a crime."

"You know that look well?"

"Stay out of my things." He said it low and barely audible.

"I'm sorry for going through your stupid bag. I just want to get out of here. My family is probably worried sick about me. Isn't your family worried about you?"

"No."

"I'm sure they are. Did you run away?"

"No."

"Then what? You just left? They're okay with you just leaving for the weekend? Spending the night in empty libraries?"

"They let me come and go as I please, and I don't turn them in for the weed they grow in the basement. It works out well."

I was stunned silent for a moment. I had heard his mom was a druggie, but it was hard to know what was rumor and what was fact. "Your parents grow weed in the basement?"

"My foster parents. Just forget I said that."

For some reason I was more surprised that it was his foster parents than I would've been if it were his real parents.

"Don't look at me like that. It's perfect. Best situation I've had yet."

Best situation he'd had yet? "I'm so sorry."

"Why? I have freedom. I'm sorry for you and your pathetically predictable life."

"Maybe I'm sorry because it's turned you into a total jerk."

"Better than a naïve, spoiled priss."

I let out a frustrated sigh. There was that word again. Why did I even try? I was not one of those girls who needed to fix broken boys. I stood up and started to walk away, but before I got too far, I marched back to his bag, opened it up, and said, "I'm borrowing your toothpaste."

His face was one part shock and one part anger when I left again, toothpaste in hand.

When I got to the bathroom I leaned my back up

against the cold tile wall and covered my face with my hand. He didn't have a phone, the only thing that had given me any hope. I really was officially stuck here.

As my breath hitched I reminded myself to focus on the good things. I had toothpaste. And a TV. I could work with that.

CHAPTER 8

• • • • • • •

As the movie credits rolled up the small screen in the break room, a memory worked its way into my mind. A couple of weeks ago a group of us had gone to the movies. Jeff, the first of our guy friends to arrive, had stepped over and around a whole row of people to sit next to me. "Is this seat saved for Lisa?" he'd asked.

It was. "No," I said, just as Lisa came in the door and saw her seat taken. I looked at her over his shoulder and she just smiled. I owed her one.

"So it was saved for me, then?"

"We'll go with that," I said, stealing a handful of his popcorn.

"First one's free," he said.

"Oh, really. And how much for another handful?"

He raised his eyebrows. "Why don't you find out?"

I hadn't followed through but changed the subject. "Where is Dallin and everyone?"

Before Jeff could answer, Dallin and the others came in, laughing.

"My mom is going to kill you," Zach said, trying to flatten his hair. "I was grounded."

"That's why we kidnapped you," Dallin said. "You get to blame us when she gets mad now."

Zach was still smashing his hair down. "Was the pillowcase necessary?"

Jeff laughed, and I glanced his way. "You didn't want to go with them to kidnap Zach?"

He shrugged. "I wanted to get here early."

What was wrong with me? I thought now, clicking off the television. Whenever I was away from Jeff, outside of our interactions, I could easily pick up on all the signs. But whenever I was near him, it was like my brain short-circuited and I couldn't tell if he liked me or not. I needed to stop thinking so much. If I hired my dad to assign me a tagline for my life, that would probably be it—*Get out of your head*. Or *It's not as bad as your brain makes it seem*. But those simple slogans were way easier said than done.

I tried to force myself to go to sleep. I was tired. My shoulders ached, my eyes throbbed, my head pounded. A nap would help. But it had been a couple of hours now since my fight with Dax, and I felt bad for calling him a jerk again. I didn't fight with people. I'd never called anyone a jerk. I hated conflict, but he seemed to bring it out in me. But with the next two days looming ahead, cold and lonely, I knew I needed to try harder to get along with him.

I was going to have to suck it up. His foster parents grew drugs in the basement of his house. That was bad enough, but I couldn't ignore the second part he'd said either. The part about how they let him come and go as he pleased. It did sound like freedom, but didn't it really mean they didn't care about him, only the money housing him brought in. I had a feeling, despite his flippant attitude about it, that he suspected that as well.

As I lay there staring at the coffee table in front of me, I noticed a little drawer. I reached forward and slid it open. A single deck of cards sat inside. I picked it up and turned it over and over again in my hands. It took me five minutes to talk myself into doing what I knew I needed to do.

I made my way downstairs. It was still light outside, and would be for another few hours. It really was warmer on this floor. *Warm* was the wrong word, actually; less cold was the better descriptor. Dax sat exactly like he had earlier. Only this time his left hand propped up his head. I could see the tattoo on his wrist now but wasn't close enough to make out what it was. He looked at me over the top of his book as though expecting me to say something.

"Hey," was my lame response.

When I didn't say anything else, he went back to reading.

Saying hi wasn't why I'd come down here. I forced the next words out. "I found a deck of cards."

He looked at the deck I had begun twisting in my hands again.

"Um . . . you want to play?"

"What game?" he asked.

I felt like if I gave the wrong answer he'd say no. "I don't care. Whatever you want."

He sighed. "You don't have to do this."

"Do what?"

"You know what."

I did know what. I felt sorry for him, and he could read it all over my face just like he'd read my disgust and fear of him the night before. Just like he knew I was going to go through his bag earlier. Was I really that transparent?

"Treat me like you always have."

"And how is that?" As far as I knew, before last night I hadn't treated him like anything.

"Ignore me. Two more days and you'll jump back on that train anyway. You might as well stay in the habit."

Ouch. "That's unfair. I didn't know you. You didn't want to be known. And I'd say you have it backward. You're the one who does the ignoring. You don't even know my name."

That last sentence must've caught him by surprise, because for the first time his hard expression dropped and he met my eyes. Without his guard up he looked younger—big brown eyes, wavy dark hair, a vulnerable look on his face. "Autumn."

Now it was my turn to look surprised. I could've sworn I was right about that. The sudden change in energy knocked the fight out of me. "Just play a stupid game with me. I'm bored."

He didn't move.

"I'm relentless."

He smiled a little. "More like annoying," he said, but he stood anyway, and we walked to one of the large oak tables.

I sat opposite him and opened the deck of cards. I shuffled them then passed them out, five each.

"What are we playing?" he asked.

"Poker. Five-card draw." My dad had guys' nights at

our house, and sometimes he'd let me sit in if a player didn't show. He'd even sneak me some cards and help me win a few rounds. I was sure everyone knew he did it, but it made us laugh.

"Okay." Dax picked up his cards, his air of confidence gone.

Maybe he was upset about his hand. I picked mine up as well. I had a pair of threes, an ace of spades, a king of hearts, and a two of clubs. Basically nothing. Should I keep a low pair or hope for another king or ace by trading in three cards?

"Do you want to trade any?" I asked.

"I . . ." He studied his hand again. "Am I trying to get the same suit or make pairs?"

I could feel my mouth drop open before I could stop it. He didn't know how to play poker? Wasn't he the one who had spent four months in juvie? Not that I knew what happened in juvie, but I'd imagined poker was one of the things. "You don't know how to play?"

"Obviously."

"Okay."

"It's not *that* shocking."

"It sort of is," I said with a laugh. "Um . . ." I'd never had to explain it before. "There are several versions of poker but this one is called five-card draw. We each get five cards."

"Hence the name."

I smiled. "Right. And then you can trade in up to three of those cards for three more from the stack."

"Do I have to trade?"

"No. Each hand is valued differently. The best hand is called a royal flush. That's when you have the same suit of a ten, jack, queen, king, and ace. You can have a straight flush . . ." I paused, realizing this was going to take forever to explain. Plus, he was staring at me with a blank face. I'd lost him.

"Maybe we should just play and I'll teach you as we go. In fact, let's just show our hands for the first couple rounds and then I'll say what I would do if I had that hand."

I placed my cards faceup on the table. "So see, I have a pair of threes and then not really much else. Ace is high card, though, so if both of us ended with the same hand, I could win with the ace. But if you had any other higher pair, you'd beat my threes. So I was thinking of keeping my face cards and trading in my threes and two. Am I making any sense?"

"Yes." He put his cards faceup. He had two sevens, two jacks, and a five.

"You punk. You already have me beat."

"So this is a good hand?"

"Well, sort of. I mean, it's really the third lowest. Seven

hands can beat it, but that's assuming I get one of those seven hands. A full house would be better. So definitely trade in your five and hope for a jack or a seven. But at this point, either way you'll probably beat my hand."

He handed me his five and I flicked him a card, faceup on top of the ones in front of him. It was a seven.

I huffed. "You lucky SOB."

"Did you just call me an SOB?"

"Sorry. That's what my dad always says to his buddies when they're playing. I forgot what it stood for until after I said it."

He looked at the card. "I take it I just upgraded my hand."

"Four slots, yes." I placed my threes and two facedown next to the stack and drew three more. I got a friend for my king but the other two were an eight and a jack. "So a pair of kings. Basically the lowest hand. You won."

"What do I win?"

"Well, if we had bet anything, you would've won the bet. But since we didn't, you win the honor of knowing you won your first hand of poker."

He didn't respond.

"So, do you *want* to play for something?" I asked, meeting his dark eyes.

"We already established that you have nothing," he said.

"We could play for secrets. Questions." I had a feeling this was the only way I was ever going to get to know Dax, because he certainly wasn't volunteering any history about himself. And despite my better judgment, I was curious about why he was the way he was—the dark, withdrawn loner.

CHAPTER 9

• • • • • • •

"Were you hustling me?" I asked after an hour of playing. We'd long ago stopped showing our hands. He'd picked up the game easily. He didn't quite know which hands beat which, or so he claimed, but that didn't matter; he was still beating me nearly every time. I was glad he'd turned down my offer of playing for secrets. "You already knew how to play, didn't you?"

"Nope."

"You hiding cards up your sleeves or something?" Without thinking, I grabbed his hand, flipped it palm up, and ran my fingers along his wrist. I could now see his tattoo clearly. Three numbers. 7, 14, 14. My finger traced the numbers without my permission . . . or his.

He met my eyes. "I don't cheat."

I pulled back my hand. "It was a joke."

He gathered his cards together and handed them back to me. "Maybe you need to shuffle better."

I started to protest but realized he was kidding when a smile played on his lips. A tingling sensation went up my arms. I rubbed at them. It was colder than I thought. "I'm a great shuffler. You're just lucky. Very, very lucky."

"You got me. I'm the luckiest guy on earth." His voice didn't sound sarcastic, but I knew he was being sarcastic. And he was right. He wasn't lucky outside of the card game. On top of that, even though he was beating me handily, this card game had been doing little for his mood. If anything, it had made him more withdrawn. I nodded toward the tattoo. "What does it stand for?"

"I have another sweatshirt."

It took me a moment to understand he was not answering my question with that statement. But when I realized I was still rubbing at my arms instead of pushing him to talk, I nodded several times quickly. "Yes. I'm cold. It's cold in here, right? Do you think there's a way to break past the locked thermostat?"

"I don't know." He stood and walked over to his bag, where he retrieved a gray sweatshirt for me.

If I'd thought that his sleeping bag was clinging to his musky scent, his sweatshirt might as well have been on his body. It smelled amazing. I slid it on and then brought the collar to my nose before I thought better of it.

"It's been in my bag a while," he said as though I was disgusted by the smell and not trying to hold back a sigh.

"No, it's good. It's fine. Thanks."

He sat back down while I dealt another hand. Now that he was avoiding my question, the only thing I could look at was his tattoo. I wondered what it stood for, why he wouldn't tell me. There were so many things I wondered about him.

I picked up my hand. It was decent for once.

"You ready to play for questions yet?" I asked.

"What do you mean?"

I folded my cards to look at him. "If I win, I get to ask you a question that you have to answer honestly. If you win, you get to ask me one."

"You do realize that I've won the last nine hands."

"Nine? Really? Have you been counting?"

"Yes."

I laughed. "Then you have nothing to lose."

He picked up his cards and looked at each one.

"So? Is that a yes?"

"Why not?"

I fanned out my cards and tried to keep my face even,

blank. "Do you want to trade any cards?"

"One."

I slid him a card then traded one as well. I couldn't help but smile when it gave me a full house. He laid down a royal flush and my smile was gone.

Before I'd even shown my cards he said, "So my question is: Where do you think your friends are? Honestly."

His question was like a punch to my gut. "How do you know you won?"

He put his forearms on the table and nodded toward my cards.

I laid them down, showing he'd guessed right. He looked at my cards, then at me again, waiting.

"I told you where I thought they were. Looking for me."

"So the whole honesty part of this bet was just for show?"

"Fine. Honestly . . . I think they figured I went home because I was tired or upset or something."

"How would you have gotten home?"

"They probably thought I called my mom or dad."

"Why would they think that?"

"Because I've done it before."

He tilted his head. "You leave events often without telling anyone?"

"I have anxiety. I panic." I'd never said that out loud

before to anyone but my parents and brother. My friends probably thought I had some sleeping problem because I generally used sleep as an excuse to leave.

"Over what?"

"Everything. Nothing. I can work through it usually. But I've learned when I can't, and that's when I leave the situation." I shuffled the cards and thought about putting an end to the game, but he'd already asked the worst question he could've; anything after this would be cake, and I was still dying to find out some things about him.

When he didn't say anything, I added, "I take medication for it. It's no big deal." My medication that was now in my overnight bag in Jeff's trunk. Missing three days wouldn't be the end of the world, but still, it was something else to worry about.

I met his eyes, daring him to make me expound some more. He didn't. I dealt another hand that he proceeded to win. I sighed and waited as he leaned back in his chair and stared me down, as if the perfect question would present itself. He had never looked at me for this long and I couldn't maintain his gaze. I began tracing the grain of the wood on the tabletop. It was pretty sad that it was this hard for him to come up with a question for me when I had a million things I wanted to know about him.

"Why are you always hiding behind your camera?"

68

"What?" My eyes shot up to his. I wasn't even sure how to answer that question because it was more of an untrue statement than a question. "I'm not. I like photography. End of story."

He nodded, then leaned back as if waiting for me to deal him another hand.

"I do. I like everything about it. I like capturing a moment in time forever. I like seeing things from a different perspective. I like taking a section out of a whole, deciding which section that is going to be. I like the predictability of a camera, that it does exactly what I tell it to do. I like capturing emotion and stories and memories."

He raised his eyebrows a bit, like that answer surprised him, but when he still didn't say anything I added, "I'm not hiding from anything."

"It's good to know what you like," he said.

"It is." How did he do that? How did he get me to say so much with so little effort? I took a deep breath, calmed my mind, and dealt another hand.

My hand was good. I only had to trade in one. When I drew the new card it gave me a full house. I kept my face as passive as possible.

He traded three and my foot tapped nervously while I waited for him to study his hand. He placed two pairs faceup on the table.

"Ha!" I said, laying my cards down. "Finally."

He folded his arms across his chest and leaned back in his chair.

There were so many questions I wanted answered that it was hard to narrow it down to one. My eyes went to his wrist. I really wanted to know what the tattoo meant, but since he'd already not answered it once, I had a strong feeling that he wouldn't answer this time either, regardless of the fact that I had just won.

Maybe he'd answer this one. "Why were you in juvie last year?"

"I thought everyone knew that story."

"I know the rumors, but I want the truth."

"You shouldn't have wasted your question. The rumors are true."

"You beat someone up?"

"Yes."

"Who? Why?" I asked.

"Foster father number three. Because he deserved it."

"What did he do?"

"He was a jerk."

"How?"

"He liked to beat on his wife. I wanted him to know how it felt. When the cops came, his wife defended him and threw me under the bus. They pressed charges."

"That sucks."

He shrugged and tossed me his cards. Then he stood abruptly. "I'm hungry." With that he left the table and headed for the doors.

I guess I was lucky he answered one question. I should've known this bet would end the game.

CHAPTER 10

• • • • • • •

Dax was in front of the television eating the rest of his candy bar when I arrived. The sleeping bag was sitting where I'd left it on the couch. I sat down on my end and pulled it over my lap.

I lifted a corner. "Do you want to share?"

"I'm good."

My candy bar was still on the coffee table, and even though my stomach wasn't protesting too much, I picked it up anyway and began eating. It was stupid to eat as a distraction here. I couldn't afford that, but I did anyway.

"I can count on one hand how many Paydays I've

eaten in my life, but right now this is the best thing I've ever tasted."

"Yeah."

"Do you eat Paydays a lot?"

"No."

"What's your favorite candy bar?"

"Do you think because we played one card game together that we're friends now?"

That took the air right out of me as a jolt of anger surged through my body "Nope. Just trying to pass the time." He probably wanted me to leave, but because he was being a jerk, I was going to stay. I laid my head on the armrest and turned my attention to the television. Some basketball game was on. I hadn't pegged him as a basketball fan. I really hadn't labeled him as anything but a troublemaker before this weekend. And he was only proving my label so far. I pulled the sleeping bag up around my shoulder.

If Lisa had been there, we'd be snuggling together, talking about our latest crushes. Just the Saturday before, we had sat on her couch, where a movie played in the background as we talked.

"When are you going to tell Jeff you like him?" she asked.

She was the only one of our friends that I'd told about Jeff. It wasn't because I didn't trust the other girls; I just spent more time with Lisa outside of school, so we talked more. "I don't know. I have a hard time opening up to him. Every time I start to, I get nervous."

"There's nothing to get nervous about. He likes you."

"He seems to like everyone."

"But he likes you the most. We've all seen it."

"Then why hasn't he asked me out?"

She squeezed my hand. "I think guys can be just as insecure as girls. You're sending him mixed signals."

"I am?"

"Yes, you'll flirt, and then when he flirts back, you back off."

"It's true. I start to overthink it. I overthink everything."

"Well, don't. You two are adorable together. And if you don't tell him, and everyone, soon, Avi will beat you to him."

"What? Avi likes him?"

"I don't know, but sometimes I think she does. Go take what's yours," she said, then laughed and laughed.

I joined her.

I came back into the present with a smile on my face. I missed Lisa. It seemed silly because I'd just seen her the day before, but I was supposed to spend the whole weekend with her. I'd been looking forward to it.

I stared at the empty wrapper in my hand. I'd eaten

the rest of my candy bar. Dax's empty wrapper was on the coffee table as well. I mentally calculated the rest of our food again. It hadn't multiplied. But we'd be fine. People survived in the wilderness for longer and with less. Why did that thought make my heart race? Why was my breathing becoming more rapid? No, I wasn't going to freak out over this.

Sometimes anxiety would hit me sideways like that, when I wasn't expecting it. When it didn't seem logical. When I thought I'd done the perfect job of talking myself through the trigger. It's like my heart wouldn't listen. I knew this whole situation was overwhelming and that my body was deciding to play catch-up, but I didn't want to do this here, in front of him. He was already judging me enough.

I stood, trying to hide my uneven breathing, and left the room. This place made me feel trapped. I needed some fresh air. There had to be a window I could open somewhere in the building. My mind raced as I remembered trying every one of those windows the night before. I went for the stairs, climbed floor after floor searching for one I hadn't tried. I arrived breathless at the very top—the fourth floor. It was a storage space of sorts. A room with boxes and boxes of stuff—old decorations, bolts of fabric, tablecloths. So much stuff. A maze of stuff trapping me.

My heart felt like it would burst from my chest. I leaned up against the nearest wall. Stop stop stop stop stop. Stop it. My eyes were watering; my ears felt plugged as my heartbeat pounded in them. I was freaking out over freaking out and that never helped. "It's okay to freak out," I said, but didn't believe myself.

I saw a door across the way—a nondescript white one with a metal bar spanning its center. One I hadn't seen before.

I tripped over my own feet as I nearly ran to it and pushed it open. The door led to a circular metal staircase. Each step creaked, and the whole staircase seemed to be a screw short as it wobbled under my weight. I held tight to the dusty handrail until I reached the top. Another door waited for me there, a creepy wooden owl on the last bit of banister watching guard over it. I yanked open the door and almost stepped onto the roof, but caught myself in time. The roof was peaked and wouldn't have been safe even without the layer of snow, but a rush of cold air hit me across the face, immediately drying the sweat that clung there. I gulped in icy breath after icy breath, cooling my insides as well.

My heart slowed; my breath evened. My legs were still shaky, though, so I lowered myself to the ground at the top of those narrow stairs and looked out at the snow-blanketed roof. Was it unreasonable to think I could sit up there for the rest of the weekend? The sky was darkening and soon the stars would be out.

I thought of being in my bed, staring at the glowing stars on my ceiling in the dark. I would be there in a couple of days, maybe sooner. I thought about the things that helped me relax—my mom brushing my hair, my dad humming while he cooked eggs at the stove, my older brother driving me to get ice cream on the weekends he came home for a visit. The rest of my body settled down with these thoughts.

I wiped at my eyes with the heels of my hands. They watered sometimes during episodes like this. It was annoying. It wasn't like this happened very often. Just once in a while when things or events I didn't expect overtook me. This situation seemed to be triggering something in me. It wasn't surprising considering how out of the ordinary the last twenty-four hours had been. I'd be back to normal as soon as this was over, I kept telling myself. I just had to get through it.

I leaned back on my palms. "Why can't I just control my mind better?" I groaned to the ceiling. No, not the ceiling. I realized I was staring at the underside of a large bell, a rope dangling down below it. This was a bell tower. Of course it was. I had seen the bell tower many times from the outside, I just hadn't thought about it at all from the inside. I was sitting in a bell tower under a bell that was never rung.

I jumped up, grabbed hold of the rope, and tugged. Someone would notice a bell that never rang, ringing. They had to.

CHAPTER 11

O r maybe nobody would notice. I'd tugged it ten times, then had gone downstairs to the main doors to wait for someone to arrive. But an hour later the outside of the library wasn't swarming with super-observant concerned citizens or hyperaware firefighters. No, the front path only held perfectly undisturbed snow.

I'd ring it twenty times. Or nonstop. Someone would hear it then. I backed up slowly from the front door, about to head up the stairs again, when a thought hit me. Firefighter. I was an idiot. This was a public library. There was a way better alarm in this place. Why hadn't I thought of it before?

★ ★ ★

A small red lever on a wall should've been easier to find. Especially since it was supposed to be findable in case of an emergency. It didn't help that it was getting dark. I had found the glass case with the fire extinguisher behind it. The one that said *In case of fire, break glass.* I assumed an alarm would sound if I broke the glass, but I felt bad doing that when there really wasn't a fire. There had to be a basic lever somewhere. Something of the non-glass-breaking variety. Maybe it was in the main room.

Dax was back in his usual spot, book in hand, when I walked in, like he'd never left. After one lap of the library, he asked, "What are you doing?"

"I have a plan." One he would probably hate, because it involved bringing the authorities right to our doorstep, but he hadn't told me why that was such a big deal anyway, so I didn't care. I went to the checkout desk and searched the underside for a panic button. Did all buildings have those or just banks?

"Are you going to share?"

"Oh, now you want a commentary?"

He didn't respond, and I was done playing his surly game. The one where he put in minimal effort and expected maximum results. I didn't have to talk either.

Kitchen! There would be a fire alarm in the kitchen for sure. That was where a fire was most likely to start in a place like this. I headed there. I heard Dax's foot-steps on the stairs behind me. That was fine with me. He could see my plan in real time.

I was right. Directly outside the kitchen on the wall was my red beacon of hope. I let out a cry of relief. But as I reached for it, I was abruptly pulled back by my hips.

"What are you doing?" he asked.

I turned to face him. "Saving us. The fire department will come and realize someone is in here and save us."

He moved between me and the fire alarm. "After breaking down the door with axes. Not to mention the alarm is probably attached to sprinklers. Is your family going to pay for the damage?"

I looked up at the ceiling. Sure enough, there were sprinklers.

"Can you really not last two more days in here? Is it that bad?"

I thought about the episode I'd just had where it felt like my heart was being ripped from my chest. I didn't want to live through another one of those. "Yes. It is. I want to go home. I doubt the alarm will set off the sprinklers. Usually there has to be smoke for that. There's a window by the front door. I'll stand there and let the firefighters know there is no fire, just trapped people. They won't break anything. They'll go get a key or something." I wasn't sure if that was true. Maybe someone would try to come in from the back or a window. But I really needed this. "Move."

"I need to be able to leave undetected. Don't do this. For me."

"We play one card game together and you think we're friends?"

He gave a breathy laugh. "I'm a jerk. We both know that, but you're not. Don't bring the fire department here."

"Why? What's the big deal? What are you hiding?"

"I'm not hiding anything. I just don't need to be on their radar."

"Why would this put you on their radar?"

"A teen *accidentally* locked in a library with his overnight bag?"

"You can say you were going to a friend's after you studied. I would've had my overnight bag here too if I hadn't put it in my friend's car."

"I have one more chance, okay?"

"What? What do you mean?"

"I don't want to end up in a group home. If I get one more strike, that's where I'm headed. I wouldn't last a day in there. They have curfews and rules. I need my freedom."

I folded my arms across my chest and let out a puff of air. "So why are you here? Really?"

He ran a hand through his hair. "Does it matter?"

"Yes. It could be the difference between me pulling that alarm when you're asleep or not."

"You're blackmailing me for information?"

"Let's call it sharing between friends."

He shook his head and a smile stole across his face. There was something very satisfying about a smile that had to be earned. It was gone as fast as it had appeared. "My stuff was on the porch. I was heading toward the canyon when it started to snow. That's it. Will you leave the alarm alone now?"

"Wait . . . what? Your foster parents put your sleeping bag and duffel on the porch?" Was that why he really didn't have a charger for his phone? Because he hadn't packed his own bag? "Why did they do that?"

"I don't know. They're probably having a members-only Tupperware party tonight. I don't ask questions. I don't care."

"At least they packed you a toothbrush." I was trying to find the positive in this when it was obvious there was nothing good about it.

"I always have my own bag packed, ready to go. I like to sleep up in the canyon sometimes. It's amazing up there. But I don't like sleeping in the snow."

"So you came here."

"Yes. Mystery solved. See, not as seedy as you probably imagined."

No, it was actually worse than I'd imagined. Who did

that? Who put a teenager out on the street to fend for himself so they could do . . . what were they doing that they didn't want him there for?

"Will the whole school know about this on Tuesday or just half?"

"No. I mean, of course not. I won't tell anyone." But maybe I should tell someone. My parents or something. He shouldn't have to live like that.

My thoughts must've been written all over my face again because he said, "Autumn. Do I look like I'm not taken care of?"

I looked him up and down. He was right. He didn't look starved. He had a lean body but it was strong. His skin was smooth, no dark circles under his eyes or anything. His hair was thick. He looked really good, in fact. Really good. My cheeks went hot and I stopped my analysis of him immediately. "No. You look . . . It's just—"

"Then let's move on. I'm fine." He pointed to the fire alarm. "Don't touch."

His story and the fact that I actually wasn't sure that the whole library wouldn't be soaked with the sprinklers if I pulled the lever made my decision for me. I could stay here. This was no big deal. He had way more to lose than I did. I held up my hands. "Fine."

"Two days. You can last two days. I have a couple of

protein bars in my bag. You can have them."

I wasn't going to eat those all by myself. I'd feel terrible. "Do you normally give yourself so little food when camping?"

"I'm normally not locked inside a building. I really hadn't planned on the library. It was a last minute decision."

I rubbed my arms. "Is this building really warmer than camping in the snow?"

He smiled.

"Can we at least try to turn up the heat?"

We stood shoulder to shoulder in front of the thermostat. Dax had used his knife to pry open the small lock. He was now pushing the On button, but it would only flash then turn back off.

"Maybe it's programmed for certain hours," he said.

"Let me try."

"You can push a button differently than me?"

I nudged him with my shoulder. "Maybe." I pushed the Up arrow several times, hoping to turn up the heat, but this time it didn't even pretend like it was trying. I flipped open the panel. On the back side were instructions on how to program it, but even following them to the letter did nothing.

"You can wear this sweatshirt too if you want." He

pulled on the front of the one he had on.

"No, that's okay. I'm fine for now. I just feel like it's only going to get colder."

"It's probably not turned off, just down. They wouldn't want the pipes to freeze."

He was right—maybe this was as cold as it would get. "I hate being cold." I turned toward him. "I especially hate cold ears. Feel them."

"Feel your ears?"

"Yes."

"Why?"

When it was obvious he wasn't going to do it himself, I took him by the wrists and directed his hands onto my ears. We were now facing each other. He was half a foot taller, and I looked up to meet his eyes. His hands felt warm, so I knew my ears must've been as cold as I knew they would be. "See. Cold."

He didn't say a word, just stared at me.

I felt stupid so I took a step back. "Socks. Maybe I can borrow a pair of your socks."

"For your ears?"

I smiled. "For my feet."

He cleared his throat and looked down at my feet and barely-there socks. "Yes." In a surprise move, he reached around me, pulled the hood of the sweatshirt onto my head and tightened the strings so I could only see out a small opening. "That should help too." There was a teasing sparkle in his eyes, one I'd never seen there before.

I laughed and shoved him, freeing myself from the hood.

A single overhead light clicked on. I hadn't realized how dark it had gotten. We'd just spent the entire day in the library. Two more and this would be over.

CHAPTER 12

· · · · · · · ·

As much as I'd wanted to sleep on the couch in the break room, it was too cold. So here we were again, on the main floor in the library, surrounded by books. Dax had loaned me a pair of socks, as well as the sleeping bag, and I was on the ground, pulling those socks as high as possible.

"What did you do with my toothpaste?" he asked from the other side of the table. Ever since I hadn't pulled the fire alarm an hour ago, Dax's expression had seemed less guarded. Like maybe he trusted me a little more now. It was a good change. It felt like we had some sort of pact, like we were on the same team now, like we were in this together.

"Oh, it's in the girls' bathroom. I'll go get it for you."

I started to get up when he stopped me with, "It's fine. I'll get it."

"You can't go in the girls' bathroom."

"Why not?" He sounded amused.

"Because . . . because . . . huh, I guess you can. We can do whatever we want. We make our own rules here!" My voice echoed through the room. I wasn't sure if it was my tiredness or boredom taking over, but I started to giggle and couldn't stop.

"Should I be worried?"

"Nope," I said through my laughter. "Go brush your teeth in the girls' bathroom. Don't mind me."

Last time I'd gotten a case of uncontrollable laughter was a couple weeks ago when my brother and I ate a whole bowl of cookie dough while my mom was on a phone call. She'd come back to help us finish baking and all the dough was gone.

"You're going to get sick. There was raw egg in that."

I'd looked at my brother and it had probably been the sheer amount of sugar we'd just ingested, but we both started laughing. When my mom continued to be irritated, we only laughed more. Eventually we'd worn her down and she had joined in.

"You're still laughing," Dax said when he came back a few minutes later. "It wasn't that funny."

"I know." I had pulled the cushions off several chairs and arranged them under the sleeping bag. I crawled inside and zipped it clear up to my chin. "But when I start, it's hard to stop."

"You do this a lot?"

"Just when I'm tired . . . or hyper . . . or happy. Oh, and sometimes when I'm nervous."

He gave a single laugh. "So the answer is yes."

"I guess so." The laughing picked up again.

He stretched out on the other side of the table from me, wadding up a shirt and placing it under his head. "But eventually it stops?"

Usually by now, the person who was witnessing my laughing spell had already joined me. Dax wasn't having it, though, which only made me laugh more. "We're stuck in a library."

"Good night." He reached up to the table between us and turned out the light.

"You're no fun." My giggling worked its way down for the next several minutes and eventually stopped.

I tried to sleep, but instead lay staring at the ceiling. Maybe it was the memory I'd just had of my mom, or the darkness that now surrounded us, but worry inched its way into my mind and crawled around freely there,

dispelling the levity of before. Worry about my parents trying to get ahold of me. Worry about my friends
thinking I had ditched them. Worry that Avi really did
like Jeff and she'd beat me to telling him at the bonfire.
My brain wouldn't shut off. I tried to distract myself by
thinking of something I could talk to Dax about.

"What would your government consist of?" I asked.

"What?" Dax answered from the blackness.

"Aside from being able to brush your teeth in the girls'
bathroom. What are your rules in our fake world?"

"Rule one. No talking once the lights go out."

I laughed. "I would veto that rule immediately."

He made a breathy sound that could've been a laugh,
but it also could've been a sigh.

"Because we're co-rulers in the library world." I
turned onto my side, propping myself on my elbow, even
though I couldn't see him. His body made a darker shape
twenty feet from me, and I tried to focus on that. "My
first rule would be games. We have to play games."

"Head games?"

I gave a single laugh. "You're good at those, but no.
Real games."

"Like poker?"

"Yes, like poker."

"You like games," he said.

"Yes." Especially games with lots of steps and

instructions where I could concentrate on those and not let my head get the better of me. Just talking about rules right now was relaxing me. Structure sometimes helped me feel safe. "What about you? What do you like?"

I thought he wasn't going to answer, which wouldn't have surprised me, but he did. "Hiking. Nature."

"And reading?"

"Yes."

"So, exploring new places?" I said.

"Yeah . . . I guess so."

"That can be rule two. You must read in the library. I mean, that rule doesn't make sense at all, but we'll keep it." He probably couldn't see my smile, but even I could hear it in my voice.

"There should be no rules in our world," he said.

"You're right. That will be rule number three."

This time he did laugh. A warm, deep laugh that made my smile double. It was the first time I'd heard it, and I hoped it wouldn't be the last. I lay back down. "Good night, Dax."

"Night."

When I woke up, Dax was already gone from his spot. I stretched. Considering I'd slept on the floor, I had slept really well. I'd been warm and comfortable. Now that I was awake, I had a slight pain in my stomach from hunger, and I had to pee, but I did not want to get out of the sleeping bag. I stayed where I was as long as I possibly could, until I couldn't hold it anymore.

After a trip to the bathroom I downed a full cup of water, hoping it would trick my stomach into thinking it wasn't hungry. It worked a little. Then I went back to the checkout desk, where I remembered seeing something the day before in my search for an alarm.

"What are you doing?" Dax asked when he came into the room and found me behind the desk digging through a wicker basket.

"This is Mother Goose's basket."

"Okay."

"She brings this to reading time every week. It has those cheapie little toys she hands out to the kids." I sifted through a few more of those toys. "Why do they call her Mother Goose anyway?"

"Mother Goose is the fake author of nursery rhymes."

"Fake author?"

"You know, like Lemony Snicket."

"Who's Lemony Snicket? And what's a fake author?"

"It's an imaginary person they attribute the writing of a book to. It makes the story seem more magical."

"Oh."

"So why are you interested in Mother Goose's toys?"

My hand closed around what I'd been looking for.

"Aha!" I held it up in the air, then threw it in the pile of the other things I'd already found.

"What is it?"

"A sticky hand."

"Okay, then." He tossed me a protein bar. "I'm going to read now."

"No. You're not. I'm bored out of my mind."

"Maybe you should sing."

My eyes shot to his. Had he heard me that first day belting out songs at the top of my lungs? Of course he had. "You know very well I can't sing."

He laughed, and my cheeks went red.

"I'm implementing rule number one," I said, changing the subject. I ripped open the wrapper of the protein bar and took a bite. "Did you already eat one of these?"

"I told you they're yours."

I broke off another piece and handed him the rest. "I can't eat all the food. I'd get a guilt headache."

"A guilt headache?"

"It's a thing."

"It must be a nice person thing." He popped the protein bar in his mouth.

"Funny."

"Rule number one?" he asked, turning his attention back to my pile of toys.

"Games. Eat, and then we compete." I gave a single

laugh. "That totally rhymed."

He rolled his eyes, but there was an amused look in them. Yes, me not pulling the fire alarm was the best thing I could have done. We were definitely on the same team now.

CHAPTER 13

• • • • • • •

We stood at the top of opposite wood staircases. He held a wrapped green Slinky and I held a red one. "Which-ever one makes it to the bottom first wins. You can only touch it if it gets stuck," I called across to him, my voice echoing in the large space.

"I could be reading right now."

"I could be eating a home-cooked meal right now, but we're both making sacrifices for the greater good."

He smiled, then tore open the plastic wrapping with his teeth. "Are you going to be as good at this as you were at poker?"

"Hey! Better to talk smack *after* you win."

We both placed our Slinkys at the top. I counted to three and we let go. His went three steps before falling between the slats of the handrail to the tile floor below. I laughed as mine kept going. "You're still in the game," I said. "You just have to get it and put it back on the same step."

He ran down the stairs faster than I would've expected and hopped the banister at the bottom. He collected his Slinky and ran back up. I'd never seen him so animated as he put his Slinky back on the step and gave it a nudge to get it going again. It was too late, though; I had directed mine to a win before his had made it another five steps. I raised both hands in the air. "Winner! Who can talk smack now?"

He folded his arms and leaned against the railing as if waiting for me to give it my best shot.

"I win because I'm the best," I said lamely.

"You've had a lot of practice, I see."

"I win all the time. I'm just humble about it."

He let out a single laugh, then scooped his Slinky up off the floor. "Best two out of three?"

"Sure. It's not like we don't have all the time in the world."

After my fifth win in a row he stood at the top of his set of stairs studying his Slinky. "Maybe mine is defective."

"Is that the excuse you're going with?"

He flipped it over and pulled on the end. "If I had a penny and some gum . . ."

I lowered my eyebrows. "What?"

"If one side was weighted I think it would go faster."

"And what would the gum be used for?"

"I'd have to stick the penny on with something."

"And *gum* was the go-to? Not tape or superglue?"

"I was trying to think of two things we might actually be able to find in this place."

"Let's move on to the next game before you start searching under tables."

"Next game?"

"Follow me."

I led him to the end of the hall, past a bronze bust of the president of the college the building used to house, then turned around. The other wrapped toys were in my pocket, and I brought out the two mini Frisbees I had found. Each had a plastic launcher.

"So you put the Frisbee in the launcher and you squeeze the end. Whichever one goes farthest wins."

"Is there a secret to make it go farther?"

"I don't know. You seem to be the one with all the secrets." When I realized how that sounded I quickly added, "I mean, pennies, gum—maybe you have some modification for this as well."

"I don't," he said.

"Well, I haven't used one of these since I was little, so I have no idea. You want a few practice rounds?" I thought he'd say no, but as he opened the package and stared at the blue disc he held, he nodded his head. I stifled a laugh. He was taking this more seriously than I thought he would.

"What?"

"Nothing."

"No, it's something. What?"

"You're competitive."

He smirked. "I'm not the one who pouted every time I lost a hand of poker."

"I did not pout."

"What do you call it, then?"

I launched my disc. "I call it showing emotions. You should try it."

"What are emotions?" He sent his disc flying down the hall as well. His landed several feet past mine. How had he done that? "So, I won?"

"No! That was a practice round. You wanted a practice round."

"Who's competitive again?"

I shoved his shoulder. "I'm not. I just like to follow the pre-established rules."

He laughed and collected our discs. "Whatever you want to call it."

When he held up his hand readying his launcher, I pushed on his arm, sending the disc flying into the wall.

He gave me a grunt, but his eyes were smiling.

I held mine up and I hadn't noticed that he'd moved around behind me until he picked me up by the waist and swung me to face the wrong direction.

"Cheater!" I called out as my disc ricocheted off the window behind us.

"I thought distractions were in the pre-established rules."

"Okay, fine, no interference this time. We launch them together."

As we held them up I kept looking at him, waiting for him to push me off balance or something. He didn't, but I *felt* off balance and sent my mini Frisbee a little too high. His was aimed perfectly by a steady, unaffected hand. He won the round.

"Is it time for rule number two to go into effect yet?" Dax asked after totally dominating several rounds of the Frisbee game.

"Rule number two?"

"Reading."

"Oh." I laughed.

"Or rule number three would work fine too."

"I vetoed rule number three. Last game." I pulled him

by his arm into the glass-enclosed walkway. The stained-glass window, the focal point of the hall, sparkled even brighter from the light reflecting off the snow-covered scenery outside. I handed him a sticky hand. "We need a tiebreaker."

"What's the game?"

"Whichever one stays stuck to the glass the longest is the winner."

"The winner of what?" he asked.

"Did you want to play for something? Another truth?"

He pinched the hand between his fingers as if testing its sticking power, then nodded. "Sure."

I counted to three and launched my hand over the rail. My red hand stuck a little higher on the curving arch of the window. His green one had a piece of the long string arm that hadn't quite stuck. I was going to win. We just had to wait it out.

"How long do they stick for?" he asked.

"My brother once threw one on the ceiling and it stayed up there for two days."

"Two days?"

"That's not the norm, though. Didn't you ever play with these as a kid?"

"No. I did not."

I sat down and leaned against the railing. I stretched my legs out in front of me.

"Nice socks," he said.

I smiled. I had pulled his socks over my jeans, and even though I knew it looked ridiculous, it was keeping me a little warmer. "Thanks. Everyone should wear them this way."

He sat down next to me, our shoulders almost touching. An electric energy seemed to radiate between us. We were probably just the only heat sources to be found in this hallway, making that energy seem like a tangible force.

"How old is your brother?" he asked.

"He's a sophomore in college. Nineteen. That makes me the youngest, with all those fun character traits."

"What traits are those?"

"Agreeable, motivated, perceptive."

"You let traits define you?"

"No. There are a lot of characteristics of youngest children that I don't relate to at all. What about you? Do you have any siblings?" Too late I realized that might've been a sore subject for him. He was in foster care. I wasn't sure how that worked if there was more than one child.

"No. Guess that gives me all the only-child traits."

"What traits are those?"

"Selfish, private, apathetic." He had a small smile on his face so I knew he was at least a little bit kidding.

"I think you mean confident, independent, highly motivated."

"You read a lot of psychology books?"

With my condition, I had, actually. "Yes, and my friend Lisa is an only child." She liked to brag about how it gave her the advantage in almost every aspect in life. *Except humility*, I always pointed out. "Do you know Lisa?"

"Is she Indian?"

"No, that's Avi. Lisa is short, has brown hair."

He shrugged. "Maybe if I saw her."

He didn't know Lisa, but he knew me? I always thought more people knew Lisa.

My eyes shifted from watching the unmoving sticky hands to the scene outside. The snow was higher than I'd seen it in a while. "Do you think that maybe cell phone reception is being affected by the weather?"

"Over a little snow? I doubt it. Why?"

"It's just, I understand why maybe my friends figured I went home and aren't worried. But I haven't called my parents in thirty-six hours now. I'm surprised they haven't been scouring the city for me. They would've called Lisa up at the cabin by now. That's where they thought I was. Lisa would've told them I wasn't there and someone would figure out I was here. I don't get it."

"Up at the cabin? Like in the mountains?"

"Yes."

"There's probably more snow up there."

"So maybe reception is worse up there?"

"It's possible. If a tower went down or something."

"If they haven't been able to get ahold of anyone, they'd just assume we were all snowed in, right? It's actually happened before—the getting snowed in part."

"There you go. Mystery solved."

"Yeah . . . I guess."

"Do you have another theory?"

"No." He was right. They were snowed in. My parents assumed I was too. Jeff hadn't opened his trunk all weekend to see my bag. It was the only thing that made sense. Lisa was probably sitting up at the cabin with Avi and Morgan, angry that I had bailed on them. We'd all laugh about this when they found out the truth. That I had spent the weekend in a big creepy library. It really was a new adventure for me.

"Where else have you spent the night?" I asked.

Dax was quiet, and I suddenly realized how that sounded without the benefit of my thought process. "I mean, when you don't stay at home and it's snowing out," I corrected.

"This isn't a weekly event or anything."

"I know, but I can tell it's not an uncommon occurrence either."

When his silence stretched on I said, "You're right, you better not tell me or I might show up at your next stop."

That comment won me a small smile.

"There's some churches that are left unlocked some-times. And I've stayed at the school before."

"Our school? Really?"

Dax shifted next to me, and his shoulder brushed against mine and then stayed there. I didn't move away.

"Yes," he said.

"Don't you ever get scared?"

"No."

"Are you scared of anything? What's the first thought that comes to your mind when I say *worst fear*?"

He seemed to think about it.

"I said first thought. No thinking, just spit it out."

"Commitment."

"Like to a girl?"

"To whatever. A girl, a cat, a class. What about you?" he asked before I could make him explain more.

"Having no control."

"Over what?"

"Boys, cats, classes."

He smiled.

"I don't know, anything, I guess. Whether a teacher calls on me in class or not. Whether my mom can keep her job. It's irrational, because I have no control over it. But that's the point, I guess. I wish I did."

My butt was numb from the cold, but I sat still, staring at the sticky hands on the glass, willing his to stay for just a few more minutes so this game would last longer. What was wrong with me? Thirty-six hours and suddenly I was craving human contact from anyone, apparently. I leaned on my right hand, breaking our connection. I could see my own breath, white puffs of air, in front of me.

Another section of Dax's sticky hand detached itself from the glass.

"Looks like mine is about to fall," he said, standing up.

"I want to win fair and square."

He backed up. "You will."

"Where are you going?" I asked as he walked away.

"Let me know who wins. I'm cold."

"You can't just leave. What if mine falls?"

"You seem like the type who would let me know that."

"I could lie."

He gave a small laugh as he continued to walk away. "No, actually, you can't."

"Just because you're freakishly good at reading facial expressions doesn't mean I can't lie," I mumbled, but he was already gone and I wasn't sure if he heard me. I wasn't sure why I was trying to claim I was an expert liar or why he made me think that should be one of my goals. It wasn't.

CHAPTER 14

● ● ● ● ● ● ●

It had taken at least another hour for his sticky hand to fall, followed by mine a couple of minutes later. By that time my hands were numb and my lungs were ice. My chin vibrated my teeth together. I grabbed both sticky hands where they had fallen down to the floor below and went back to the main library. It didn't feel much warmer.

"I w-won," I stuttered out to his reading form, then dropped into the nearest chair, plopping both the toy hands on the table. "In your face."

He smiled. "You're getting better at smack talk." He

had the sleeping bag around him. He took it off and held it out for me. When I didn't move, he got up and walked it over.

"Was it worth it?" he asked, dropping it in my lap.

"Depends on your truth."

"Oh, right, what's your question?" He went back to his chair.

What was my question? Wasn't this why I'd waited so long in that icy hall? I'd really wanted another truth out of him. There were so many questions I could ask—how was I supposed to narrow it down to one?

"I'm not all that interesting," he said when I was quiet for too long.

"Just a mystery," I responded, causing him to laugh. I really did like his laugh.

"How so?"

"You're always alone, you disappear during lunch, you never talk, not even in class, and you don't seem to care what anyone thinks of you."

"And here I thought you hadn't been paying attention."

"You're hard to ignore." When I realized how that sounded, I added, "Everyone is always talking about you." My statement went from bad to worse. I stopped while I was ahead.

"Right. So was there a question in there somewhere?"

"Where are your parents?"

When he flinched a little, I knew I was the most insensitive person ever. What made me think I had earned that information, even if we were on the same team now? "You don't have to tell me. I can think of another question."

"My dad is physically absent and my mom is mentally absent."

I must've looked confused because he clarified. "My dad left when I was little. My mom is a drug addict."

"I'm sorry."

"Don't be. Like I told you before, I am perfectly fine. I am in a really good situation. And next year, I'll be officially free of the entire system."

He had nobody. Nobody he could count on when he was in trouble, nobody to help him if he made the wrong step or lost his way. He was all alone. My eyes burned with tears that I held back.

He sighed. "Don't assign me emotions. Don't pretend to know what I'm thinking based on your experiences."

I tried to control my expression even more. I needed to take him at his word. He said he was fine. He was probably fine. I was giving him emotions based on my universe, not his. "I'm sorry."

"Don't be." He picked up his book again and read.

★ ★ ★

It had been hours. I was wrapped up in the sleeping bag and my teeth still hadn't stopped chattering. I wondered if it was the lack of food. Did the body need food to warm itself? What had I been thinking staying in that cold hallway for so long? Dax didn't seem cold at all, sitting there in his chair reading away.

"D-Dax." My throat hurt.

"Yeah?"

"What are the symptoms of hypothermia? Because I can no longer feel my fingers."

He glanced up at me, then back down. "Go run the stairs or something."

"Run the stairs . . ." He was right. I just needed to get my blood pumping. I stood and walked toward the stairs. Stars appeared in my vision for a moment, my head light. But I maintained my balance and made it to the stairs. The hallway was dark, the sun setting. I had been in the library for another full day. Just one more full day to go. Plus two nights . . . Why did that sound like an eternity?

I started the steps slow, just walking up each one. As the feeling returned to my extremities, I picked up my pace. My mind began to wander. I missed my friends. Especially Jeff. He made me laugh. Just the week before he'd come into the yearbook room, where I was arranging the Clubs page on the computer. He'd sat down, took one look at the page I'd spent the last thirty minutes on, and said, "Looks perfect, now let's go."

"Does it really? I'm not sure if this one is very good."

He had barely given it a glance. "All your pictures are awesome. Now come with me." He pulled me up by the arm and led me away.

"I need to save my work."

"Someone will save it for you. You need to take me to the teachers' lounge and buy me a soda."

"We're not allowed in the teachers' lounge."

He stopped in front of the door leading there. "*I'm* not allowed in the teachers' lounge. But you can go anywhere you want, it seems. Teachers like you. With you by my side, I could do anything."

"I'm not going into the teachers' lounge."

He laughed and then knocked. I gasped, my heart racing.

The vice principal opened the door. "Can I help you?"

"Autumn wants a soda," he said.

"No, I . . ." I started through my tight throat.

"Hold on a second." She shut the door and I shot Jeff a look.

"Are you trying to get me in trouble?"

"Don't worry. No trouble here."

He had been right. She came back a minute later holding a Coke. When she shut the door again I laughed.

"See, teachers love you."

"Oh please. You wrote the book on how to charm teachers. Obviously."

He smiled.

My socked foot slipped on a stair, jolting me out of my memory and nearly sending me falling. I caught hold of the rail, preventing that fate. My stomach let out a large growl and I wondered if physical activity was going to make me warmer but hungrier. I headed to the kitchen and decided the mystery dish needed to be warmed up and attempted. The only thing I'd had that day was half of a protein bar, and that was hours ago.

The microwave took me a while to decipher. I overcooked it a bit, hoping that would kill any bacteria that might've been living in the old food. I tried not to think about that as I forked a small bite into my mouth. It tasted like pasta with marinara sauce and it was very good. I wasn't sure if that was because I hadn't eaten anything real in a while or if it actually was good, but I took a few more bites anyway.

I ate exactly half and took the rest down to Dax.

"You braved the unknown?" he asked, accepting the dish and looking in the bowl like he wasn't sure he was willing to do the same. He sniffed at it.

"Yes. It's good. Eat it."

The food and the exercise had done the trick for me, and my chin had finally stopped shivering. Dax put his book to the side and took a small bite.

"What do you think it is?" I asked.

"Pasta? Very overdone pasta."

"It tasted good to me. Probably because I'm hungry."

He took another bite, then held out the bowl. "You can have the rest. I don't like it."

"Really? You're a food critic now?"

"Yes. And that's disgusting."

I grabbed the pasta and it wasn't until I ate two big bites that it occurred to me what he'd just done. Did he just pretend not to like it so I could eat it? Because this wasn't gross at all. I wasn't sure one way or the other. It didn't seem like something he'd do, but then again, he was different than I'd originally thought.

"Have you ever been to that Italian place on Center Street? Gloria's or something?" I asked.

"No."

"Because you don't like Italian food?"

"It's not my favorite."

Huh. Maybe he really didn't like it. I finished off the rest and put the empty dish down. "You should work on your history project while you're here. We finished ours on Friday."

"Yeah. Good idea." I could tell that was the last thing he was going to do. I wondered how his grades in school were. He missed so much I couldn't imagine him doing very well.

"I can help you if you want."

"Sure. You get started. I'll join you in a couple hours."

I kicked his foot with a smile. "Funny."

I walked over to the pile of books I had thrown the first night. Some were open facedown, their pages bent. I picked them up one by one, smoothing out the pages and stacking them neatly. Then I walked them over to a cart at the end of an aisle. There were several books already on the cart, waiting to be put away. Books with titles like: *Ten Steps to Rehabilitation*, *Habits of an Addict*, *Brain Chemistry and Addiction*. They weren't necessarily Dax's books—they could've been anyone's, but Dax had been here Friday too, obviously, waiting for the library to close. Was this the research he was doing instead of Mr. Garcia's project?

He doesn't want your pity, I reminded myself.

"I'm getting ready for bed," I told him, then turned around and headed for the bathroom, where he'd started leaving all the toiletries he'd brought. I took my time getting ready and then tucked myself into his sleeping bag.

CHAPTER 15

· · · · · · · ·

I awoke to a sound I couldn't quite place at first. A clicking of sorts. It took me several disorienting minutes to realize it was Dax, twenty feet away from me, shivering in his sleep. Had he been holding back his shivering when he was awake for my sake? I tried to ignore it, knowing he wouldn't want me to do anything, but I felt guilty. I had the very thing he had brought to keep himself warm. I climbed out of the sleeping bag, unzipped it and crawled over to him, dragging it behind me.

When I reached his side, I draped half of it over him and kept the other half. He immediately woke up . . . or maybe he hadn't been fully asleep to begin with.

"I'm fine," he muttered.

"That seems to be your mantra. Just take half."

"I don't need it."

"Shut up and take it."

He didn't argue and finally stopped fighting it. He was cold. We weren't even touching but the temperature under the bag noticeably dropped with his icy presence.

He chuckled a little.

"What?"

"Have you ever told anyone to shut up?"

"Nope. It's like you pull it out of me."

"How did it feel?" he asked.

"Good, actually."

He laughed again and I inched a little closer, knowing my body heat would warm him up even faster.

We were quiet for several breaths. Breaths that I could see like a mist above us as we both lay on our backs. We had been in the library for two full days and even though I felt like we had some sort of pact, I wondered if he would acknowledge me outside this situation. "Are we friends yet?"

"I don't have friends."

I nodded even though I was pretty sure he couldn't see me.

"But . . . you're less annoying than I imagined you'd be."

"Thanks." That was probably the closest he would ever come to giving a compliment, but I was still offended. I didn't want him to know that so I added, "You imagined me often?"

It had been a joke, but the way he went still beside me made me think that maybe there was some truth to it.

"Yes, all the time."

"I thought so," I said, pretending I didn't know he was being sarcastic.

"Is it hard for you to think someone might not like you?"

"Yes, actually."

"Why do you care what people think so much?"

I thought about that question. Why did I care? Because I liked it when people were happy. Because I didn't like to think that someone might not like me? "I don't know." I took a deep breath. "I'm going to sleep now that your teeth aren't chattering anymore."

"My teeth weren't chattering."

"They totally were. Apparently you do have some feelings as much as you try to deny them."

He didn't say anything back, so I said, "Good night."

"Night."

I inched even closer, because his body still felt cold, and tried to sleep. My mind wouldn't shut off. Five minutes passed, then ten. The second hand on the wall clock sounded like a drum beat.

I wished I didn't care what people thought about me. "Why don't you care?"

"What?"

"What people think about you?"

"Because I have no say in what other people do . . . or think."

"I guess it's hard for me to accept I don't have a little say over that. I mean, the things I do can change people's opinions."

"If my mom taught me one thing it's that you can't control anyone but yourself."

The mention of his mom brought me out of my own issues. I thought about those books sitting on the cart on the other end of the library. If he'd really given up thinking he could help her, he wouldn't have been reading those books. *If* he was reading those books. They might've been someone else's. Dax's mom wasn't the only drug addict in Utah. "If you're in foster care with the weed-basement parents, where is your mom? Getting help for her addiction so you can live with her again?"

He let out a breathy laugh. "She'd have to want to get better before she got help."

"Can she work?"

"She holds odd jobs off and on."

"When's the last time you saw her?"

He shrugged, his shoulder brushing mine, we were so close. "It's been a while."

"I'm sorry. That sucks."

"Could be worse."

"Could be better."

"It always could."

"Wow. So much positivity."

"Yes, you know my reputation, the poster child for optimism. It must be an only child thing."

I smiled. "I'm sorry," I said again, because I didn't know what else to say.

"It's life."

But it wasn't. Well, it wasn't everyone's life. I wished it weren't his.

I rolled onto my side, facing him. I knew I was close but I hadn't anticipated that the movement would close the rest of the distance between us. I pretended like it was purposeful and put my hand on his chest. "I'm still cold," I said, hoping he'd accept my closeness if it were me suffering and not the other way around. He did give up food for me, after all (or so I suspected). I was glad he couldn't see my face because he'd be able to read the truth.

He rubbed my upper arm without a word, as if that action alone would warm me.

I rested my cheek on his shoulder, wondering what had gotten into me. How had he made me so relaxed? How could I say whatever I was thinking to him? Do whatever I was feeling? Maybe because he was the only one around, I thought with a small smile.

He adjusted his position so his arm was under my head, his hand now resting on my back. My heart picked up speed. Dax didn't have any reaction to my nearness. His breathing was normal, and so was his heartbeat—I could tell, because with my ear against his chest now, it was loud.

"Do you know Jeff?" I asked.

"Your boyfriend?"

"He's not my boyfriend."

"Yet?" he said, using the same word I had earlier.

"Right. Do you know him?"

"I thought we already established that I didn't know anyone."

"I thought maybe he'd been in one of your classes before."

"Why?" he asked.

"Just wondering."

"Just reminding yourself you have a boyfriend?" He paused, then laughed. "Or were you reminding me? You're the one who came over here."

My cheeks flooded with heat. "No. I wasn't . . . no. I just wondered what you thought of him."

"Of Jeff? Why do you care what I think of him?"

"I don't know. I don't. Never mind."

It was quiet for several minutes and I thought maybe

he was on his way to sleep when he said, "Jeff seems nice. He was in my English class last year. He was never a tool to me."

That thought made me smile. "He is nice." I closed my eyes. After a few moments of silence, Dax's breathing became a steady rhythm, lifting my head slightly with every intake. I could feel myself drifting when he adjusted his left arm and his wrist came into view. *7 14 14.* "What does your tattoo stand for?" I whispered. If he was already asleep, if he didn't hear me, I'd let it go. And I thought he hadn't heard me.

Then he said, "Independence day."

I was surprised he answered at all. I wondered if he was half asleep, his guard not fully engaged. "I think you're a few days off on that."

"My independence day. The day I let go of caring, of worrying, of everything. The day I first tasted freedom."

He made it sound like a good day, but what he described made me sad. It sounded like it was the day he realized he was alone in the world. How could that be a good day? I knew he didn't want my pity, though, so I didn't offer it. "Did something happen on that day to make you realize that?"

"Yes," was all he said.

"Freedom, huh? So when you're eighteen and graduated you want to leave here?"

"Yes."

"Where do you want to go?"

"Anywhere. Knowing I can leave when I want, that nothing is holding me here, is the only thing that keeps me sane. It's why a group home would kill me."

Silence hung around us. His shivering had finally stopped. I thought about moving away now that he was warmer, but I couldn't. "I won't tell anyone you were here."

"Thank you," he whispered.

I smiled. He did know those words.

CHAPTER 16

The weight of Dax's arm draped across my waist held me in place the next morning. I didn't want to move and wake him up. I was on my right side, facing away from him. He was behind me, his breath warm on the back of my neck. I tried to control the goose bumps that were forming up and down my arms.

It was the first morning I'd woken up before him. It was our last full day here. In about twenty-four hours, someone would unlock those doors and we'd be free.

Dax stirred next to me and I closed my eyes again so it didn't seem like I'd been lying there awake this whole time, enjoying his arm around me. At first, his hold around my waist tightened and he took a deep breath, then, as if he realized what he was doing, he cursed quietly and backed away. The cold air bit into my skin, a wake-up call to more than just one of my senses. I could not in any way become attached to the guy who'd just told me the night before he didn't form attachments. He had a tattoo on his arm branding him a loner. What made me think I would be any different to him than anyone else? I wasn't. We were just trying to make the best of a weird situation we'd been thrown into together. This was all temporary. When we were out, everything would be back to normal.

I stretched and sat up. My stomach let out a long growl. I put my hand over it and laughed.

He smiled, something he'd been doing more readily than he had before, dug out the last protein bar from his bag, and threw it to me.

"What's the first thing you're going to eat when we leave tomorrow?" I asked.

"Donuts."

"Plural?"

"At least five."

"I've been missing salt, not sweets. So maybe a burger and fries."

"That sounds good too."

"Everything sounds good," I said, taking half the protein bar and handing back the rest. "Well, except this."

He ate the remaining half in one bite. "It's definitely not donuts," he said through his mouthful.

"Ooh, a burger, fries, and a shake. That would satisfy both cravings."

He nodded.

"There's that burger place two blocks from here. We should walk straight there when the librarians unlock the door."

He wadded the paper from the bar into a ball and rolled it between his palms.

"We can pack up all our things—well, your things— wait behind that pillar down by the parking garage and as soon as they pass by, sneak out."

He tilted his head at me.

"What?"

"You're going to sneak out of here when people show up?"

"What else am I going to do? Sit here and wait for them to find me? Then I'd have to explain everything. They'd call my parents. I'd have to wait for them to show up and explain everything again. That would take forever. I'm starving."

He laughed. A sound I still wasn't used to. "Food is definitely top priority."

"Higher than the top," I said. "Oh! Have you ever had cronuts?"

"Cronuts? No."

"It's a croissant and donut combined. They are the best things in the world. I'm going to buy you a cronut when we get out of here. Oh no . . ."

"What?"

"We don't have any money. How are we going to buy anything without money?" I thought for a moment. "I have money at my house. It's only, like, five minutes from here. We'll hitchhike to my house, get money, and go eat."

"Hitchhike?"

"Or we can borrow the phone at the gas station and have Lisa pick us up. That's what we'll do. Or we can beg for money. Like hold up a sign on the street corner. That's a good idea too."

"Sounds like a plan," he said.

I stood and stretched again. "We'll figure something out. We will be eating food at the earliest possible time tomorrow." And then I'd see what price I was going to have to pay for this weekend. I crossed my fingers that my parents just figured we were snowed in and I had no way to get ahold of them. If for even a second they were worried, I'd have a lot of explaining to do, and I wanted to do that explaining on a full stomach.

These thoughts took my mood down several notches. "I'm going to get a drink." I waited for him to say something about how he didn't need to know my every move, but he didn't. Maybe he was used to having another person around at this point.

I took a long drink of water, then went to the bathroom and brushed my teeth. My hair was a mess, my face was completely makeup-free now, and sure enough, I had a zit forming on my chin. But it didn't matter to me at all. I was relaxed around Dax. He'd become a friend. As much as he didn't want one, he now had one in me. His tough guy act wouldn't work on me anymore.

I went back to the main room to see it empty. Where had he gone? I may have been in the habit of giving him my play-by-play, but he obviously wasn't yet. Maybe he was in the bathroom.

His book lay abandoned on the chair—*Hamlet*. I picked it up and flipped it open to the page he'd left off on and read a few lines. I'd never read *Hamlet* before. When I went to shut it, I saw what he'd been using for a bookmark. An envelope—addressed, stamped, and ready to be sent. But it was obvious it had been ready for a while, its edges bent, a fold down the middle. I read who it was supposed to go to—Susanna Miller. His mom? An aunt, maybe? Who was Dax afraid to reach out to?

I shut the book and placed it back on the chair, then

went to the checkout desk. Why didn't the librarians have a secret food stash somewhere? I started going through the drawers behind the counter when I found a big bag of the little toys they must've used to refill Mother Goose's basket. I lifted the sealed bag and tried to see it from all angles; maybe there was candy in there. I tucked the entire thing under my arm and went upstairs.

In the break room I turned on a movie, opened the plastic bag, and began looking through it.

Dax arrived half an hour later, and I was laid out on the couch with his sleeping bag spread over me. He held up his Frisbee in the launcher and shot. It hit the side of my head because I was too lazy to free my arms and stop it.

"Ouch," I said with a laugh.

"Sorry, I was aiming for your shoulder."

"So your aim's not perfect after all."

He stood by the arm of the couch closest to my feet and waited for me to scoot over.

"But I'm comfortable," I joked, and just as I was about to sit up to give him room, he picked up my feet and sat on the cushion beneath them, letting my legs fall onto his lap.

Despite my earlier declaration to myself that we were going to be friends, I was surprised by the gesture. I hadn't thought he was quite caught up with my future plans yet. Maybe he was.

"What's all that?" he asked, pointing to the layer of individually wrapped toys spread across the coffee table.

"Not candy. That's what it is. Don't librarians know that kids like candy?"

He smiled.

I reached over to the table and picked up one of the items that was not candy. It was a black bracelet made of thread. "Give me your wrist."

"What?"

I held up my hand and eventually he placed his in my palm. Then I tied the bracelet onto his wrist. "There. Now you have a memento of our time in the library."

"You expect me to wear this?"

"Yes. Forever."

His eyes scanned the table until they stopped on something that he plucked from the pile. A bracelet like the one he wore but hot pink. He held out his hand.

"Pink? No way. Find me a black one too."

He didn't move, his hand waiting there. I growled but relented. He tied a careful knot, then turned his attention to the movie.

I turned my attention back to the movie too—*Pirates of the Caribbean*—a smile on my face.

"Johnny Depp or Orlando Bloom?" I asked.

"Johnny," he replied, without asking me to clarify my statement.

"Yeah, me too." Johnny always plays eccentric roles, different roles, ones that help me feel like no matter what my issues, there's a place for everyone in the world. Dax's hand moved from the back of the couch to rest on top of my ankle. And in this moment, I felt like this was my place.

CHAPTER 17

•   •   •   •   •   •   •

When the movie was over, I sat up and stretched. "I'll be right back," I said.

As I reached the door, Dax asked, "Where are you going?"

I turned to see a smirk on his face. "Do you really want to know?"

"Not at all."

I laughed and left without telling him, even though I was sure he actually was curious. I went to the kitchen and grabbed the little corner of cake from the fridge, then brought it back to the break room.

I cleared away some of the toys, set the cake on the coffee table, and sat down next to him, pulling half of the sleeping bag back over our legs. The cake sat under a plastic dome that I hoped had kept it fresh for however long it had been there. Dax had found a new station on the television and I focused on it.

"What are we watching now?"

"Some documentary on Martin Luther King, Jr."

"Oh right. It's Martin Luther King Day. I almost forgot."

"Which is why the library is closed."

"Right. We're going to miss part of school tomorrow," I said.

"Tragic."

I missed my fair share of school days to anxiety, but this one felt different. "You miss a lot of school. Why?"

"I always have a reason," he said.

"That was vague and cryptic. You like those kind of answers, don't you?"

He bumped his knee into mine under the sleeping bag and I wasn't sure if it was on purpose or an accident. He probably thought that was a good answer to my question.

He nodded his head toward the cake. "Did you bring that in for torture or were you planning on eating it?"

"Did you want cake, Dax?"

"Yes."

I laughed, sat forward, and attempted to pry off the cover. It was nearly impossible. Dax didn't move to help and I sensed him silently mocking me.

"I'm eating this whole piece when I get the lid off."

"But then you'll get a guilt headache."

I finally freed the cake, got a finger full of frosting, and smeared it across his cheek.

He tried to give me a serious look but it dissolved into a smile. "Really?" He left the frosting there as I broke the cake in half and ate my portion. It was so sweet it made my cheeks hurt. He ate his half as well, frosting still on his face.

"Are you going to wipe that off?" I asked.

"Nope."

A stack of napkins sat on the table and I handed him one.

"But then it won't bother you anymore."

"You think you know me so well now, huh? Well, you don't. It doesn't bother me at all."

He turned his attention to the television, acting like he didn't even feel the frosting there.

I sighed and wiped it off myself. I met his stare while I did, my hand on his face, our bodies close, and my heart seemed to stop.

I sat back, threw the napkin onto the coffee table, and positioned myself under the sleeping bag before I did something stupid. "Well, you're nearly impossible to get to know, but you know that already. You do it on purpose," I said.

"I do very little on purpose."

"I find that hard to believe."

His hand, which was resting on the cushion between us under the sleeping bag, brushed against mine. I had a strange urge to grab hold of it, but I fought it. His leg bumped mine again, but this time stayed, pressed against me, the pressure of it making my brain go soft.

"But, with very little help from you, I think I know you pretty well now too," I said.

"Oh yeah?"

The volume of the television went up even though neither of us had touched the remote. The news had come on and it was louder than the previous program had been. "Leading the news today, we have an update on the story we brought to you last night out of Utah County. One missing, presumed dead, one injured after the car he was driving crashed in American Fork Canyon Friday night, plunging into the river. Jeff Matson was on his way home from a party with friends. It's unclear whether alcohol was involved in the accident." I gasped as my picture came up on the screen. "Autumn Collins, a senior at Timpanogos High School, hasn't been found. Her belongings were pulled from Matson's car after he was rushed to the hospital in critical condition. The river has been searched over the last several days. Authorities are worried, given the state she'd have been in after the crash and the low temperatures, that she didn't survive the accident. Search parties have been scouring the woods bordering the river, but the search was called off last night as another snowstorm pummeled the area. Matson remains in critical condition at Primary Children's Hospital in Salt Lake."

A voice sounded by my ear. "You need to breathe. Deep breaths."

I gasped in a breath. My heart was racing and blood rushed through my ears.

"If you have any information regarding this ongoing search," the woman on screen continued, "please call the police department."

My parents thought I was dead. Pressure built up in my chest, pain taking over. My eyes hadn't left the television screen even though they had moved onto another story. I was frozen to the couch, incapable of knowing what to do next. I wasn't even sure I remembered how to move. That's when a loud buzzer began to sound, causing my ears to ring. The noise ripped through the room and beyond, over and over, like my alarm clock in the morning. And just like my alarm clock, I wanted it to stop. I threw my hands over my ears, wondering where the noise was coming from. Was it in my head?

"Are you having a panic attack?" I heard a distant

voice ask from beside me. "What do you normally do when you have one?" He was rubbing my back.

My brain was too muddled to think straight. This was worse than anything I'd ever felt before. I needed fresh air. I needed to see my parents. My brother. The people who right now thought I was dead. This wasn't happening.

"I have to get out of here," I said over and over and over. I couldn't stop myself from saying it.

"Autumn. You need to breathe. Put your head in between your knees or something."

"Why?" The world around me was going black.

"Autumn, look at me."

I met his eyes. They were intense and focused and more serious than I'd seen them before.

"You are going to pass out if you don't slow down your breathing."

"I. Don't. Pass. Out," I said between breaths.

"Maybe you haven't before, but I'm guessing you've never had a panic attack on an empty stomach."

I couldn't get enough air into my lungs. "I have to get out of here."

"I know. They're coming. Someone is on their way. Hang on."

Before I could analyze what that meant, everything went black.

CHAPTER 18

• • • • • • •

"Can you hear me? Open your eyes."

It felt like I was crawling out of a black hole and I really didn't want to put in the effort. It would be easier to stay at the bottom and sleep. But something was itching the bridge of my nose and around my mouth, and I wanted it to stop. I tried to touch my face but my arm was pushed back down.

"Can you tell me your name? What day it is?"

I opened my eyes and immediately shut them against the brightness, then attempted to blink until the sting was gone. I was in the back of an ambulance. A black

137

woman stood over me, her hair pulled back, a smile on. "Hey. Welcome back."

"Autumn. It's Autumn."

"Actually, it's winter."

I pushed at the oxygen mask and tried to sit up.

She gently forced me back down by my shoulder. "Just lie there until we get to the hospital and the doctor can check you out."

My memory was coming back to me. Of what I saw on the news. My stomach hurt. I searched for Dax in the space around me but only saw tubes hanging off the walls and plastic boxes presumably full of first-aid supplies. On my other side sat a red-headed guy with a clipboard. Dax must've been able to escape when the ambulance showed up. That thought helped me relax. I didn't want him to get in trouble, like he was sure he would if any officials were involved.

I stayed lying down but was able to pull the mask off my mouth. "No. My name is Autumn. It's January something. Martin Luther King, Jr. Day. I don't remember the exact date. I was trapped in the library. Do you have a phone I can use to call my parents?"

"What's the phone number? We'll have them meet us at the hospital."

"Thank you."

★ ★ ★

My mom didn't normally cry, so it surprised me to see the tears in her eyes. It made me cry too. We were crying for different reasons. She cried because her daughter was not dead. I did because I felt terrible that she'd thought I was. She held me so tight for so long that finally the doctor had to tell her that he needed to put in an IV for the dehydration.

"Mom, I'm fine."

She took a deep breath, and I watched her bring herself under control, dab her eyes, and straighten up. "I know, you'll be fine." She turned to the doctor as the nurse readied the needle beside me. "When can she come home?"

"As soon as she drains that liter of saline and we check her vitals again."

My mom nodded.

The nurse pointed at my sweatshirt. "Can you take that off, please, so I can put your IV in?"

I'd forgotten I was wearing Dax's sweatshirt. The thought had me looking at my feet where I still wore his socks, up over my jeans. While my mom's back was turned, I pulled my jeans out and over the top of them. And instead of taking off the sweatshirt, like the nurse had asked, I pushed up the sleeve. I was still cold. "Does that work?"

She nodded as she studied my left arm, searching for

the perfect vein. I looked away as she brought the needle up and distracted myself by talking to my mom.

"Where is Dad?"

"On his way."

I sucked air between my teeth when the needle went in. The nurse taped it in place.

"Does anyone have my shoes?" I asked.

The nurse and doctor exchanged a look that ended with both of them shaking their heads no. "We'll check out front," the nurse said. Then both she and the doctor left us alone.

"They're probably still at the library," my mom said. "I doubt anyone thought to bring your shoes."

I could picture exactly where they had been, tucked under the chair next to Dax's bag. Maybe he had grabbed them when he snuck out. I'd have to ask him about that at school.

"You're more concerned about your shoes than your phone?" my mom asked. "Impressive."

"Right. My phone." I didn't want to think about that bag in the back of Jeff's car and what had become of it. But I knew I had to. Now that I had explained everything and my mom seemed to be calming down, it was time to find out about Jeff.

Before I could say anything, though, my older brother, Owen, walked in, followed by my dad, cutting off the question on my tongue. The one about Jeff.

"What are you doing here?" I asked Owen. "What about school?"

"It's a holiday. Thankfully you were presumed dead on a holiday or I'd be missing chem lab for this." Right, it was a holiday, and of course my brother would drive six hours from UNLV if he thought I was dead.

Mom smacked his arm. "Stop being so flippant about this. This is serious."

"It's not serious anymore," he said, giving me a hug. "I'm glad you're not dead."

"Yeah, me too."

He held on to me and wouldn't let go until I pushed him away with a laugh.

My dad sat on the edge of my bed. "What happened?"

I had to explain the whole situation again. The only thing I left out was Dax. I'd promised him I wouldn't tell anyone he was there and I planned to follow through with that promise.

"How are you feeling now, kid?" my dad asked.

"Starving. A milk shake and fries would probably cure me," I said, batting my lashes at him.

He tousled my hair. "Sounds like you're fine."

"I would feel better with a milk shake too," Owen said. "I mean, my sister was dead this morning."

My dad looked up in thought. "How about this for a

slogan? Milk shakes: Cure the shock of thinking a loved one is dead."

My mom rolled her eyes. "Vance, you're as bad as the kids."

"Come on, Owen," Dad said. "Milk shakes for everyone." They left, Owen throwing me a thumbs-up over his shoulder.

My mom gripped my hand so hard that my fingers were turning white. I didn't have the heart to ask her to loosen her hold. I shifted on the bed, the stiff hospital sheets itching my skin. The doctor said I could leave once the entire bag of saline hanging next to my bed was emptied into my arm; I was guessing that would take a while, though, since it wasn't even a quarter of the way gone.

"Mom," I said, not wanting to ask the question I knew I needed to. I didn't want to hear the answer. I wanted to pretend everything was fine now that I was out of the library. "How is Jeff? Have you heard anything?"

"Last I heard, still critical. I haven't checked in since yesterday. I've been involved with the search party."

"Search party?" It took me too long to remember she was referring to me. "Oh. Right."

Her eyes shone with held-back tears.

"I'm sorry, Mom."

"It's not your fault. I'm so happy you're okay."

"But Jeff . . ." Now tears were stinging my eyes.

"I'm sorry, honey."

"He'll be okay, right?"

She patted my hand, finally softening her grip, but didn't answer my question.

"Can I see him? Is he here somewhere?"

"He's in Salt Lake in intensive care. Only family can see him."

I nodded. Maybe I could send over flowers or something. Maybe I could call the hospital and they'd tell me how he was. They'd tell me he was fine. Because he was going to be fine.

I stared at the clear bag full of saline until the door opened a crack and a white cup appeared.

I smiled. "Look who came to visit me. Milk shake."

My mom turned in her chair. "Come in, Vance, before the doctor sees what you've smuggled in here."

My dad came in, followed by my brother, who held his own milk shake. "I will smuggle anything anywhere for my only daughter."

I took a long drink. "How many days do I get the we're-just-happy-you're-alive parents? I need to know how long I have to take advantage of you."

My mom tried to give me a serious look but only ended up trying to gain control of her emotions again.

Owen rolled his eyes and mouthed *way to go* at me behind Mom's back.

"Okay, fine, I won't take advantage of you if it means you'll stop crying."

"I'm just so happy," she said.

My dad put one hand on my shoulder.

"I know," I said. I knew they were relieved now, their lives righted. But for me, it felt like the real tragedy had just begun. I tried to keep my happy face in place for them.

My family weren't my only hospital visitors. Before I could drain that liter of saline, Lisa, Avi, and Morgan had stopped by as well, saying they had heard the news when the day's search was called off.

"I thought you left with Jeff," Lisa whispered as the others talked to my parents. "I thought for sure you had. We hadn't even started the fire when it started to snow pretty bad. We had all just gotten there and decided to head up to the cabin before we needed chains for the cars. Jeff left first."

"Why would you think I left without telling you?"

"I don't know. It was crazy. Avi was screaming about being wet. Everyone was laughing. I had been pressuring you to tell Jeff at the bonfire. I thought you left with him. And you know what I thought to myself? I thought, 'Go Autumn.' I was proud of you. And then I heard the news and I was devastated. It was my fault you were with him."

"I wasn't with him."

"I know, but I thought you were, and it was my fault. I'm sorry."

I shook my head. "Lisa. Stop. Even if I had been with him, it wouldn't have been your fault. It was an accident." I took a deep breath. "Thank goodness nobody was with him."

"I know. Only girls had jumped in his car on the way to the bonfire and they were all continuing on to the cabin."

"But Jeff," I said.

"I know. Believe me, I know."

"Have you been to see him?"

"He's in the ICU. No visitors."

I sighed. I couldn't get worked up about him before I knew anything. Lisa's face looked how I felt—etched in worry. My face must've looked the same, because she slid next to me and wrapped her arms around my waist.

"I'm just so relieved you're okay," she said.

"I was never in danger. I was fine."

She laid her head on my shoulder. "I'm sorry I left you in the library. I'm an idiot."

I shook my head. "No, please. Don't worry about that. It's my fault for drinking half a two-liter bottle of DP."

She tugged on the sleeve of my sweatshirt. "Whose is this?"

I remembered how easy it was for Dax to read my lies and tried to channel calm when I said, "I found it at the library. It was so cold there."

She took a big whiff of me. "It smells good. Like . . ."

Dax. It smelled like Dax.

"Man," she said, and I laughed. "It smells like a guy. Like a really good-smelling guy."

"I thought the same thing when I put it on."

She sat up. "Were you terrified in there?"

I twisted the hot pink bracelet that was still tied around my wrist. "It wasn't too bad."

"You'll have to tell me all about it when you get out of here."

"I will." And I would. I'd tell her everything in a couple of weeks, when all of this had died down and everyone was done asking questions. When Jeff was out of intensive care and fine. When enough time had passed for Dax to see he wasn't going to get in trouble for this. Then I'd tell her.

CHAPTER 19

At six o'clock the next morning my eyes popped open for the eleventh time since I'd closed them the night before. My mind was filling my dreams with worry. Worry about Jeff, about Dax, about my parents. My bed was too soft, too warm. The house in general felt very warm. Had my parents turned up the heat higher than normal?

I climbed out of bed, my head pounding when I stood up. I needed aspirin.

I was surprised when I found my mom sitting in the recliner in the living room, her laptop open on the arm of a chair and a legal pad on her lap. "What are you doing? Did you sleep out here?" I asked.

"No. I couldn't sleep. I'm researching the protocol on nighttime procedures for public buildings."

"Mom."

"You shouldn't have been locked in there. Every room should've been searched before the last person left."

"Mom, can you not do that?"

She sighed. "I keep thinking that I dreamed yesterday. That I'll wake up and you'll be . . ."

"You didn't. I'm here. I'm fine." I felt guilty once again for not pulling the fire alarm earlier. That's how we were eventually discovered, my mom had told me— the fire alarm. Dax must've pulled it.

I kissed the top of my mom's head, then continued on into the kitchen. "Did Owen make it back to school okay?"

"Yes, he texted me at about one a.m."

Another thing to feel guilty about—making my brother drive six hours to help search for me.

"What are you doing awake?" my mom asked.

"Couldn't sleep either. Plus it's time to get ready for school."

"You're not going to school." It wasn't a question.

"I am. I feel fine and I need to get my mind off things. Plus I don't want to fall behind." I had been reaching for the bottle of aspirin while giving my speech and stopped myself short. If Mom saw me taking aspirin, she definitely wouldn't let me go. I grabbed my anxiety medication and a glass instead, just as she joined me in the kitchen.

I could practically see her having an internal fight with herself before she finally said, "Okay, but you come home if you start to feel sick or anxious at all."

My head throbbed to the rhythm of my heartbeat as I filled the glass with water from the fridge. "I will, Mom."

I hadn't anticipated the reaction that would take place when I walked into the halls of school. It was the last thing on my mind. But I should've known. My face had been all over the news and social media. I had been presumed dead. Of course the kids at school would know. I opened the door and stepped inside, and before the door had even shut behind me, a couple of people cheered and said hi.

"Hey," I answered back.

A guy from my Government class stepped in front of me. "Welcome back."

"Thanks?"

"Autumn!" Cooper Black, a defensive lineman on the football team yelled. "You survived!"

"Survived?" This was going to get old very fast.

My friends were just as bad. Lisa, Morgan, and Avi acted like they hadn't just seen me the day before at the hospital and smashed me into a group hug. "You came to school today! I didn't think you'd come," Lisa said.

Well, that explained their reaction. Then Dallin, Jeff's best friend, barreled into me. He lifted me over his shoulder and carried me down the hall yelling, "She's alive! She's alive!" His reaction confused me most of all. I thought I'd find him a mess today, since Jeff was still in critical condition, but he seemed like his normal self.

During my unasked-for ride, I caught a glimpse of Dax walking down the hall. My heart jumped into my throat and I knew he was the real reason I'd come to school today—to make sure he was okay. Just as I lifted my hand to wave, he looked away, not acknowledging me at all. By the time Dallin had carried me to the end of the hall, my head was pounding even more than it had been that morning. I hit his back. "Let me down, Dallin. Please."

He did, nearly plopping me on my backside in his effort. Then he gripped me by the shoulders. "We should have a Back From the Dead party this weekend on your behalf. Zombie-themed or something."

I grabbed onto both his wrists. "How are you?" I asked sincerely.

He smiled and dropped his hands back to his sides. "Awesome. Ready to celebrate."

I narrowed my eyes, wondering if he was more worried about Jeff than he was letting on. "No party for me this weekend. I just want a break."

He wiggled his eyebrows. "We'll see about that." Then he ran off, probably to start the early invites to a party I didn't want.

Lisa plopped into the seat next to me in sixth period—Government. "Where were you at lunch?"

"Avoiding people." And looking for Dax. Since the initial sighting that morning, I hadn't been able to find him again. Was this how he was going to play it? We were just supposed to go back to normal, like we didn't know each other at all?

"You look tired."

"I am. I should've stayed home."

"You should just wear a sign for the next week that says 'Touch me and I'll put an ugly pic of you in the yearbook.'"

I smiled. "Think that'll work?"

"That's the ultimate threat, Autumn. Use your power."

I pulled my binder and a pen out of my backpack because Mrs. Harris started writing on the whiteboard. "I want to go to the hospital today after school and talk to Jeff's parents. Take them flowers or something."

"Do you know his parents?"

"I met them at his pool party last summer. I feel like I need to do something."

"Me too. I'll come with you."

"Thank you." I was hoping she'd say that. I still wasn't sure what I would say to his parents. *You probably don't remember me but I should've been in that car with your son? Sorry I wasn't with him when he plummeted forty feet into a river?* Those would make great icebreakers.

"They'll probably be happy to see some of his friends."

"They'll tell us how he is, right?" I asked.

"I hope so."

Mrs. Harris clapped her hands twice. "Okay, class, get to work on these questions, then we'll discuss."

CHAPTER 20

• • • • • • •

"These flowers feel too cheery, too bright," I said, unable to get out of the car even though Lisa had turned off the engine two minutes ago and the car was slowly transitioning to cold.

"I think that's the point. We're not going to a funeral, Autumn."

I groaned. "I know." My palms were sweating. I took several deep breaths. He was fine. Jeff was fine. I pulled on the door handle and pushed open the door. "Let's go."

The lady at the information desk pointed the way to

the intensive care unit waiting room, warning us that's as far as we'd make it if we weren't family. I was okay with that.

Lisa grabbed my hand as we turned the last corner.

I recognized Jeff's parents immediately from the summer before—both tall and handsome, like Jeff. They sat in the corner of the room, a few others I didn't recognize around them. It seemed as though their bodies and the chairs they sat in had become one, like they'd been there for years. A television was on in the corner but nobody was watching it. My chest tightened another notch.

"We shouldn't be here. I feel like I'm intruding," I whispered. "You think they'll be mad at me that I'm fine and he's . . . ?"

Lisa pulled on my arm, forcing me to face her. "You've done nothing wrong. I think they'll be happy that you care about Jeff and you're here to check on him. You're breaking up the monotony of their day."

"You're right."

"Of course I'm right." She walked forward, pulling me with her.

Jeff's mom barely glanced at Lisa before meeting my eyes. The stem of one of the daisies in my hand snapped. I loosened my hold.

She stood, her hands going to her mouth. Jeff's dad looked at her and then followed her gaze to me. He offered a shaky smile. Then Jeff's mom was weaving past chairs and people until she stood in front of me. I felt seconds away from passing out even though I had only ever passed out the one time.

I held out the flowers lamely, unable to speak. Lisa saved me.

"Mrs. Matson, we are so sorry about Jeff and just wanted to come and say that we were thinking about him."

Even though Lisa had been the one talking, Mrs. Matson's hazel eyes hadn't left mine and they crinkled with a smile. "Autumn," she said.

So she did remember me. "Yes, hi."

She gripped me by my shoulders, the flowers still held out between us. "Autumn."

This was getting weird. I nodded.

"I'm so happy you're here. Jeff thinks the world of you."

"He does?" I'd always hoped he was talking about me to someone. I never imagined it was his mom.

She pulled me into a hug, her chin digging into my forehead. The flowers, which I'd only slightly destroyed before, were now crushed. When she let go, still not acknowledging Lisa, she began dragging me toward the waiting group. I helplessly followed, giving Lisa a look that said, *please don't abandon me.* She read it well and stayed close on my heels.

"Jason," Mrs. Matson said when we reached her husband. "This is Autumn."

A barely-there smile appeared on his face. "Yes, I remember you from a party at our house, nice to see you."

I held out the now limp flowers, hoping someone would take them from me. He did.

"Thank you."

"Autumn wants to see Jeff," Mrs. Matson said out loud.

"Oh. No, that's okay, I know it's family only. I just wanted to find out how he was doing."

"Yes, it's family only, cousin Autumn," Mrs. Matson said, giving me a wink.

"What?" I don't know why I said that. I got her implication immediately. I was just shocked. Why would she want me to see Jeff?

My own question was answered minutes later, after Lisa had given me a shrug, after Mr. Matson had gone along with the lie, his dark eyebrows only rising slightly in surprise, after I'd made it past the nurse with the cousin story despite my sweaty palms. Mrs. Matson linked her elbow with mine conspiratorially as we followed the nurse down a long white corridor. She whispered, "These first few days are very important for Jeff. They've put him in a medically induced coma until some of the swelling in his brain has gone down. Maybe his girlfriend is just the medicine he needs."

"No . . . I mean we're not . . . we never even . . . we're not together."

"I know, but it was only a matter of time, right?"

I swallowed hard. Yes, it was only a matter of time. I liked him. So I could forget about the pressure I felt right now to be what his mom needed me to be—some sort of miracle worker. I could try to shake off the jitters I always felt about seeing someone sick and helpless. Right now he needed me. We stopped outside a door and the nurse pushed it open. His mom smiled my way, and we all stepped inside.

The room was quiet except for a beep from the machine next to his bed that sounded in a steady rhythm. But even that became distant as I took Jeff in. There was a long gash on his forehead that was stitched up and surrounded by what looked like iodine. There were heart monitor pads on his chest and a tube coming out of his mouth. His eyes were swollen and there were a few scrapes on his arms. I tried not to let the stinging in my eyes turn into tears.

"Go sit next to him. Let him hear your voice," his mother said.

This woman had seen too many movies.

"We can't stay long," she continued. "They like to let his mind rest, and too much excitement in the room seems to raise his heart rate. But you have a few minutes."

A few minutes was more than enough. My heart rate was high enough for the both of us.

She nudged me toward the chair at his bedside. "Don't be afraid to touch him."

I sat and looked at his arm, not sure if I wanted to. But she was standing beside me, full of hope. So I reached out and placed my hand on an open patch of skin between a scrape and the IV. I did want Jeff to know his friends were here and thinking about him.

"Hey, Jeff. It's Autumn." I felt self-conscious speaking to him with an audience.

His mom must've sensed this because she said, "We'll give you a couple minutes." Then she told the nurse she had a few questions and they went out into the hall.

I waited for the door to shut, then cleared my throat. "Hey. I came to see you." I wasn't sure what else to say but went on anyway. "You don't look too bad. Only slightly worse than that time you went through the car wash without your car." I laughed a little, remembering that day. We'd seen an empty field of mud as we were driving home from lunch. Lisa had said something about how it was too bad we hadn't taken her four-wheel drive. Jeff got that mischievous gleam in his eye and said, "Who needs a four-wheel drive?" Then he'd proceeded to drive donuts in it. Only he'd forgotten to roll up his window. So not only did his car get a mud bath, he did as well. That's when he got the idea to walk through the car wash at the gas station before heading back to school. The bristles left a few scratches on his face, and he came out looking like a drowned rat.

"Remember that, Jeff? The car wash? One of your many brilliant ideas that turned out not to be quite as brilliant as you thought it would. You need to wake up and make me laugh. I had a crappy weekend. Sure, not as crappy as yours, but still." I squeezed his arm, then dropped my hand to my lap. "You're going to be fine. Lisa is here too. She came to see you. But she's not your cousin like I am, so . . ." I sighed. "Jokes aren't as funny to tell when you can't hear them."

It was nice to see him, to hear the beeps that represented his heartbeat, see his chest rise and fall, even though I knew a machine was making that happen. He was alive, and I was grateful for that.

When we walked back into the waiting room, Lisa attached her arm to mine and didn't let go. Jeff's mom hugged me and whispered, "Come back soon, please."

"I don't want to take family time," I said.

"No, please." She squeezed my shoulders a little too intensely. "Let me get your phone number so I can give you updates."

We exchanged numbers, and I said, "I'll come back as soon as I can."

Lisa tugged me away and we were silent as we walked

to the car. It wasn't until we were inside with the doors shut and the engine running that she said, "How was Jeff?"

"I don't know. Okay, I guess. I mean, he's in the ICU, so I'm sure there's a lot of internal stuff going on, but he looked like he could get up and walk out of there if he wanted to."

"Are you okay?"

I was wondering the same thing, waiting for the tears I'd been holding back to finally come. I kept them in even though my throat and chest hurt. "I think so."

Lisa nodded and looked over her shoulder to back out of the parking space. When we were on the road, driving toward my house, she said, "That was weird that his mom made you go in there. Like you possess some sort of healing power."

"I know. Really weird."

"When are you going back?"

"I don't know. This week sometime. I need to be there for him . . . and maybe his mom, too." I sighed. "I feel guilty."

"What? Why?"

"The same reason you felt guilty when you thought I was in the car with him."

"Him being there is not your fault."

I put both my feet up on her dashboard, hugging my

knees to my chest. "If it weren't for me, he wouldn't have been in the canyon that day. I feel guilty that he might have gone over that cliff thinking that I hadn't wanted to see him at the bonfire. That I'd gone home instead."

"Autumn, you got locked in a library. It wasn't your fault."

"Maybe not, but I can be there for him now."

Lisa smiled. "Maybe you really can help him. His mom acted like you were the love of his life." She shoved my shoulder. "He must've talked about you a lot."

My cheeks went hot and I hid my face against my knees. "Shut up."

She laughed. "You love it. Autumn and Jeff. It's so happening."

An image flashed into my mind, not one of Jeff healed and walking out of that hospital with me, but one of Dax's eyes, staring at me across the library. I pushed it out. "Yes, it is happening." It would happen. It had always been what I wanted.

CHAPTER 21

• • • • • • •

If I could just talk to Dax and make sure he was okay, maybe my mind would stop thinking about him when it wasn't supposed to. Plus, we were friends now and I was worried about him. I wanted him to sit with us for lunch, hang out with my friends, not be alone. I wasn't sure he'd get along with my friends, but it was worth a try. I couldn't find him anywhere at school, though. It was like he had this superpower to vanish off the face of the earth whenever he wanted to.

At lunch, I scanned the cafeteria as I sat with my friends. Not that I'd ever seen Dax there before, but it was worth a look. He wasn't exactly predictable.

Dallin was making a party-planning list. "What are other foods that remind you of the undead?" he asked.

Lisa held up a carrot stick. "These are sort of undead-like. Fingers or something."

"I meant *good* food," Dallin said.

Avi snatched Lisa's carrot stick and took a bite. "I heard some girl in my English class talking about this party. How many people did you invite?"

"How many people *didn't* I invite is the question."

The idea of being surrounded by mostly strangers with loud music in a crowded house made my insides tense. "Dallin. I don't want a party."

"Well, that's all well and good, but that's past decided. I need your input on food now."

"This sounds like a lot of effort," Zach said. "Can't we just bring whatever and call it good?"

Dallin pointed at him. "Yes, I like this plan better."

Lisa rolled her eyes. "Are your parents cool with this?"

"Yes, I told them I was doing it to celebrate Autumn's return, and they were fine."

"Don't use me as an excuse to throw a party," I said.

He laughed. "I will use any excuse I can think of."

"When is this thing, anyway?"

"Saturday. So you better be there or my parents will think I lied."

"Ugh." I shoved his arm.

Avi laughed. "I have that emotion ten times a day in regard to Dallin."

The bell rang. I scooped my lunch trash into my brown paper bag and headed for the trash can. "You're dead to me," I said to him as I went.

"You're undead to me, baby."

Lisa jumped up to join me and we headed toward Government together.

"Has he been to the hospital?" I asked.

"Dallin?"

"Yes."

"I think so."

"Is he in denial about Jeff or overly optimistic?"

"I think this is just the way he's dealing with it."

I stepped over a lunch tray that was left on the floor by the exit. "Yeah, probably."

"But is there a reason you're not optimistic about Jeff's recovery?"

Because Mrs. Matson said he was in a medically induced coma. That meant the doctors were worried, didn't it? But how would it help my friends to know that? "No. He'll be fine. I just don't feel like throwing a party right now."

"We have to celebrate the little things, right?"

I smiled. "My return from the dead is now a little thing?"

She laughed. "So small. I mean, come on, you were only locked in the library."

I smiled and hip-checked her. I could suck up my reservations and let my friends throw a party. Maybe it was just what they all needed. Some hope.

The laundry was stacked in piles on the coffee table when I came through the front door after school. I grabbed the two piles that were mine and headed for my room to drop them off.

"Autumn," my dad said, cutting me off in the hall, holding another basket of laundry.

"Oh, hi. I wanted to ask if I could go to the hospital again today."

"Weren't you just there yesterday?"

"Yes, but . . ." I paused when I saw that he was holding Dax's sweatshirt.

He must've seen my gaze because he said, "Is this yours?"

I went with the lie I'd already started on Lisa. "I found it in the lost and found at the library. It was cold in there. I'll just take it." I grabbed it from him but he didn't relinquish it right away.

"Maybe we should return it."

"I can do that," I said, finally tugging it free. I draped it over my arm and continued walking with the two stacks I already had.

"I thought maybe it was that boy's," he said.

I came to an abrupt stop and turned around quickly, the sweatshirt slipping off my arm and falling in a heap at my feet. "What boy?"

"The one the doctor said was with you when the paramedics arrived."

I was stunned silent.

"Maybe he heard the alarm too," my dad said. "Was able to get into the library somehow to help you. I didn't get all the details. But I think the police got his info."

"Police?"

He chuckled a little. "You really were out of it, weren't you?" He ran a hand along my cheek. "I'm glad you're okay now. I'd like to thank that boy and get more details. Maybe I'll call and find out how."

Maybe *I'd* call and find out how too. Dax could avoid me at school, but he wouldn't be able to avoid me if I showed up on his doorstep.

It had taken a couple of phone calls but I'd finally been able to talk a police officer into telling me the address Dax had given them. I now stood on the porch at his house wiping my palms, which were starting to sweat, on my jeans.

The door opened with a squeak, and a woman not much older than thirty answered. Her hair was multicolored and she wore an oversize T-shirt and jeans. "Can I help you?"

"Hi. Is Dax here?"

"Is he in some sort of trouble?"

"No, I just want to talk to him."

Her eyes traveled the length of me. "He doesn't live here anymore."

My mouth opened, then shut again. "What? Where does he live?"

"Who are you?"

I shifted on my feet and put on a smile even though I didn't have the best feelings for this woman. "A friend. I have some of his things."

One thing really, his sweatshirt, and it was just a convenient excuse to see him.

"What things? They're probably mine. He took a lot of my things."

"They're not yours. Do you have his address?" I was getting more irritated by the second.

"CPS didn't tell me. I just know he was going to some group home."

I closed my eyes and took a calming breath. So he had been sent to a group home over this. Over helping me. "I think you know where that home is, but maybe I should call CPS and let them know about the extra income you grow in your basement." Did I just say that?

"Are you threatening me, girl?"

Fear snaked up my spine. I'd never done anything like this before, and I was sure it showed on my face, but I was getting desperate. "Yes."

She mumbled something to herself and slammed the door in my face.

I let out a frustrated growl, then kicked her door. I just needed to walk away and forget about this. Dax got himself into this mess by deviating from the plan. He would be fine. He'd be eighteen soon, and then he could walk away from everyone like he'd always wanted.

I needed to get to the hospital. That's where my dad had agreed I could go. That's where I should've been. I turned and had just descended the two cracking cement steps toward my car when the door creaked open. The woman threw a crumpled piece of paper at me and immediately shut it again. She locked it as well.

I stared at the paper sitting on the porch next to the doormat shaped like a flower and a tipped-over green plastic watering can. I picked it up, smoothed it flat, and smiled at the address written there. I probably shouldn't have been so happy about blackmailing information out of someone, but considering the victim, I didn't feel quite so bad. I'd found him. And he never needed to know how.

CHAPTER 22

• • • • • • •

The group home caregiver was a tall black man with a pleasant smile, unlike Dax's last foster parent. He also looked like he'd actually gotten ready that morning versus rolled out of bed. He had the early stages of a beard along his jaw, but his head was as smooth as could be.

"You're here to see Dax?"

"Yes."

He looked at his watch. "He'll have to go over his schedule with you. Now is homework. He has free time after four."

Dax would hate that, I was sure, his life scheduled to the minute. I checked my phone. It was 3:45. "Do I have to wait or can he get done a little early today since I didn't know?"

"Just this once. Let me get him."

"Thanks." I clutched his sweatshirt in my hand. A moth clung to the wood around the door frame and I watched as it moved its wings without flying.

Dax came to the door, his hair disheveled, wearing a wrinkled tee and some athletic shorts. His feet were bare, and around his wrist was the black bracelet I had tied there.

My tight chest loosened. I wanted to push up the sleeve of my sweater and show him I was still wearing mine, too. I didn't. I held out his sweatshirt. "Thought I'd return that."

He took it and I had the strangest urge to grab it back, hold on to it, keep it.

"And my socks?" he asked.

"Oh. Right. I forgot about those. I'll bring them next time."

"It's okay. You can keep them."

"Did you happen to grab my shoes?" When he looked confused I added, "They were black ankle boot wedges."

He laughed. "Because that clears things up."

"You can't picture them perfectly now?"

"No, I didn't get them. They're probably still at the library."

Right. Still at the library.

Dax stood in the open doorway, as though ready to shut the door without a second thought. I searched my brain for another reason to keep him from doing that.

"So a group home, huh?" was the idiotic solution my brain came up with.

He looked at the door. "Dreams do come true."

"You were supposed to leave."

"What?"

"When people came, you were supposed to hide and then leave. It's what we talked about."

"You're mad at me for waiting when you were passed out?"

I realized I *was* mad. He was here, where he didn't want to be, and it was all his fault. "Yes. You should've left."

He laughed a little. "Glad you think me capable of leaving a girl passed out on the floor."

"I would've been fine. They would've found me. But now everything is a mess and you're here and you're miserable."

"Autumn, stop. No need for guilt. I won't be here for long."

I wished I had his ability to read facial expressions, because his was so stoic I couldn't tell if what he said was the truth.

"But I don't understand, why would they punish you for helping me?"

"My foster mom said I ran away for the weekend so she wouldn't get in trouble for kicking me out."

"My dad didn't know you were with me. He thought you came with the alarm."

"I gave minimal information to the police. CPS doled out this awesome punishment."

I groaned. "This sucks."

He shrugged. "It's fine."

"How come you haven't been at school?"

"I've been around."

"I thought you could sit with us at lunch . . . if you wanted to."

That was the wrong thing to say. His face went from the Dax I'd come to know, to closed off again. Like I'd pushed a reset button. "I don't need you to set me up with friends, Autumn. I'm fine." The hallway behind him was dark and seemed to be swallowing him up. "I better get back to mandatory homework time."

I didn't want him to leave feeling like however he now felt. I needed him to stay for just a little bit longer, so I blurted out, "Jeff's in a coma. They won't bring him out of it until he's doing better."

That stopped his backward movement again. "I'm sorry."

"His mom thinks I am the key to saving him."

"What do you mean?"

"She pretended I was his cousin and I sat by him and talked to him and she wants me to come back and do the same thing. Like I have some magic touch or something." I laughed nervously, surprised I had told him that. "It's no big deal, though. Maybe I can help."

"You don't have to go back, Autumn."

My shoulders relaxed a notch. "I want to."

"I hope he gets better."

"Me too." I toed the corner of the doormat. "If you ever need a break . . . I have a car." When he didn't say anything I added, "You can borrow it or something." Maybe Dax didn't want to hang out with my friends, but we were still friends. He was still wearing the bracelet, after all. That had to mean something. And as his friend, I knew things about him, like the fact that he'd need some freedom from this place once in a while. A car helped with that.

"Borrow your car? I'm sure your parents would love that."

"They'd be cool with it." They would not be cool with it.

"I don't need your car, but thanks." He moved his hand up on the door, his expression seeming to ask if I was done with my outbursts yet.

I bit my lip. "Okay . . . well . . . good luck with everything."

"You too."

I took a step backward. "Bye, Dax."

"Bye."

He shut the door and that was it.

I started to leave but then hesitated, thinking I'd left something, my arms felt empty, but then I remembered it was just his sweatshirt so I hopped off the porch and drove away. Maybe that bracelet didn't mean anything, after all. Dax didn't need my friendship. He didn't need anything. Now that I saw that, I could stop worrying about him.

CHAPTER 23

• • • • • • •

My dad was sitting on the couch matching socks when I came in the door. The television was on (which explained why the task was taking him so long) and he paused it to say, "How was the hospital?"

"I didn't end up going. I dropped off that sweatshirt instead." That wasn't a lie, even though I knew he would assume I went to the library.

"Oh good. Dax. His name is Dax." He searched the pile of socks on the coffee table for the right one.

"What?"

"The police told me who the boy who helped you

was. I wrote him a letter that they said they'd send to him for us."

"That's great."

He held up a finger as if he just thought of an idea. "Did you want to add anything to it?"

"The letter?"

"Yes."

I smiled, thinking that could be funny. "Sure, Dad."

He swept the socks off his lap and onto the cushion next to him, then led the way into the kitchen, where he took a folded sheet of paper out of an envelope. I read through the words, which mainly talked about how grateful he was that Dax heard the alarm and came to help me. How this act let him know Dax had a strong character. I picked up the black pen on the counter and added the words, *My hero* then signed my name.

My dad read it, a crease forming between his brows. "That doesn't seem very sincere."

"It is."

He folded up the letter and stuffed it back in the envelope.

I wondered if I should've added more. My words were supposed to be funny, but they sounded bitter. I was still angry with him for getting caught, I realized, for brushing me off at the house, and at school for that matter, for being able to close the door so easily.

"I have some photo homework to do. Can I go down

to the park for a little bit?"

"Sure."

In my room, I slung my camera bag over my shoulder, grabbed my jacket and scarf, and headed to the garage for my bike. When I was shooting outdoors, it was so much easier to travel on my bike than in the car.

I stopped at the park up the street. Even with snow still on the ground, it was full of bundled-up kids. I dropped my bike by the racks, traipsed through the slush, and found a group of bare trees.

As I brought my camera up to my eye, I let out a sigh. It had been too long since I'd looked at the world through the lens. It helped clarify things for me, straighten out my thinking. Looking at the harsh angles of the bare tree, its background bleak, I knew I was letting my life get blurry. I needed to focus on what mattered—Jeff.

Lisa didn't go to the hospital with me this time, and as I walked into the lobby I wondered if it was a mistake to go alone. It was too late to change my mind now—Mrs. Matson had just caught my eye across the room. She jumped up faster than I thought possible, stopping mid-sentence with the lady next to her to race toward me.

"Autumn! I'm so happy you're back. The best thing happened after you left the other day! He squeezed my hand."

"He's awake?"

"No, not awake yet, but that's the first time there was a sign that there is that possibility."

"That's great."

"It was you."

I stared at her for a long moment before I said, "No. It was your hand he squeezed. I'm sure it was you. He didn't move at all for me."

"I'd been here days and nothing. You were here minutes and . . ." She trailed off and hugged me. "You are like a miracle. You came back from the dead and now you're here to share the good karma."

"I wasn't dead."

She ignored my statement. "They're going to stop the medicine that's keeping him under now. See if he'll wake up."

"They are? That's amazing."

"When he wakes up they'll be able to assess things more. See the extent of his injuries. Come on. You need to see him."

His eyes were less swollen today, although now that the swelling was down I could see the discoloration around them more clearly. Just like the other day, she left me in the room with him. I sat down, and it was like my body remembered exactly how it was supposed to act in here because it was immediately back on high alert. *Stop it*, I told my body. *You're fine. Look where* he *is.*

"Hey, Jeff. What have you been up to?" I smiled. "I know, my jokes are getting lamer." I put my hand on his arm again. "I bet you're so bored. I mean, if you are aware at all. I should read to you or something. Is that what is customary when a friend is in your situation? It seems like that always happens in the movies. What would you even like to read? I don't think I know that about you." If I were honest, I didn't know that many meaningful things about Jeff. I mean, I knew the same things everyone else who hung out with him knew—he liked baseball and practical jokes and was very smart—but it wasn't like we'd ever had a deep conversation.

"Maybe I should ask your mom if you have a journal. I could read that to you. Unless you want to object. No?" I sighed. "Sorry, they really are getting lamer."

I looked back over my shoulder, toward the door. It had been a couple of minutes. I was surprised his mom hadn't come in to tell me that time was up yet. This was all the time I had gotten before. Maybe longer visits had been approved in the last forty-eight hours. Because he squeezed a hand. I stared at his hand for a moment and then placed my palm beneath it. "Jeff? Can you hear me?" I closed my hand around his, then held my breath as I waited to feel something back.

Nothing.

"There's a basketball game tonight," I told him. "Lisa

and everyone went. They said to say hi. I'm supposed to go over there after this."

I traced the red nurses'-call button on the side of his bed with my finger. "Remember when you wanted to try out for mascot and you got that threatening 'anonymous' letter that we all knew was from last year's mascot? And then you walked around telling everyone that you were still going to try out even though it was now life or death for you." I laughed. "That was nice of you not to in the end. Did you even really want to or had it always been a joke?" These were the kinds of things I should've asked him before. The kinds of things that didn't seem important but now that I was thinking about them, actually would've told me a lot about who he was . . . is. These were the things I was going to ask him when he woke up. Why *hadn't* I asked him these questions before? I was interested in him. Shouldn't I have wanted to know everything about him?

"I don't think I'd want to be a mascot. I'd be too self-conscious in front of everyone like that. You'd make a good timber wolf, though, because I'm pretty sure you love to be the center of attention. And you never seem to worry what anyone thinks. I wonder if the costume is super hot. I'd get claustrophobic. Did you know that about me, that I get panicky in small places? Where don't I get panicky, though, right?"

That was the closest I'd come to telling my friends about my anxiety. I rolled my eyes. "You can't count that as telling him, Autumn. He's in a coma," I mumbled under my breath.

My stomach let out a large growl and I covered it. My phone said it was seven. I let my eyes wander around, take in each machine, the white walls, the ticking clock. My stomach growled again, so I stood. "I'll see you Monday, Jeff."

I sent a quick text to his mom. Yes, I was avoiding her. She would want a progress report and I hated having nothing good to tell her. Mostly, though, I just needed to get out of there.

CHAPTER 24

• • • • • • •

The music was too loud when I started my car, and it made me jump. I quickly turned it down and drove out of the parking lot and toward the school. Just the thought of the basketball game made my insides twist. I didn't want to go. It was going to be loud and crowded and overwhelming. I didn't know if I could handle that right after leaving the hospital. But I told my friends I would, so I knew I had to. I could always leave later.

By the time I arrived at the game it was more than half over. I found Lisa, Avi, and Morgan in the middle of the bleachers, their cheeks painted with a red number 4.

I laughed. "You are all supporting Wyatt? How is he going to choose between you?" Wyatt was the star of the basketball team. I'd taken his picture for yearbook, but outside of that we'd only interacted minimally.

"We'll share," Avi said right before standing up and screaming as our team scored two points.

I tried to get into the game, but the gym felt extra packed tonight and louder than usual. It made my chest vibrate and my eyes water.

"You okay?" Lisa asked next to my ear.

I had put my elbows on my knees and my head in my hands. "Yes," I said. "I'm just worried about Jeff."

"Let me know if worrying works and I'll jump on board."

I smiled over at her. "Sometimes I feel like it will."

She put her hand on my back. "Just think about the milk shakes we'll be drinking in thirty minutes. Those are the answer to every problem."

Maybe milk shakes *were* the answer to every problem, because the second we stepped inside Iceberg, things seemed much better. Quieter at least. I ordered a large chocolate shake and fries. As I sat down with my order, I remembered this was a meal Dax and I had talked about eating upon our escape.

"Why are you smiling?" Lisa asked, sitting down next to me in the booth.

"Because this is excellent."

"Isn't it?"

I hadn't had the chance to talk to Lisa about Dax yet, but I could now. After all, the worst had already happened: Dax was in a group home. Me telling Lisa wouldn't change anything now. "And . . ."

"And what?"

"At the library—"

"Dax Miller," she said.

"What? How did you . . ." I stopped when I saw her looking at the door.

My eyes immediately followed her gaze to where Dax and a couple of other people were walking to the counter. My heart skipped a beat.

"Who's he with?" Lisa asked. "I've never seen him with anyone. Is that his dad? His dad is black?"

"Does Dax look black to you?"

"Maybe he's adopted, or half. You never know."

"It's his foster dad." Or group home dad, I wasn't sure what his official title was, but it was the man who had answered the door and gotten Dax for me when I went to his house the other day. He was talking to the cashier, then handing over his credit card.

I sat there, on edge, my shake clutched in my hands,

waiting for Dax to turn and look. I could wave. He could wave back. That would show me he wasn't trying to brush me off like it seemed he was the other day on his porch.

He finally turned, but his eyes just scanned the room, only pausing on me for a second before they moved on. Total brush-off. I sat back in my seat. No wonder he had no friends.

CHAPTER 25

• • • • • • •

"We're not supposed to dress like the undead for this party, are we?" Morgan asked, holding up several shirts as she looked in the mirror. It was Saturday. Lisa, Avi, and I had arrived at Morgan's house an hour before and were well into getting ready.

"I hope not," I said.

"It wouldn't surprise me if Dallin and Zach and the guys did," Lisa said.

"You're right. They so will."

I sat on the floor in front of the full-length mirror, applying mascara. It was weird to think that the Saturday before I'd been in the library. It felt like a lifetime ago. I almost wished I were there right now instead of on my way to a party. My head was still throbbing from the basketball game and the hospital the night before.

"So I call dibs on Wyatt and Sawyer tonight," Morgan said.

"You can't call dibs on two people," Avi said.

"I just did."

Lisa laughed. "That's fine with me. There will be plenty of others for us."

Morgan gave me a sad face.

"What?" I asked.

"I'm sorry Jeff won't be there for you."

Jeff. Why were we having a party again? It felt so wrong. "He'll be better soon enough. Then Dallin will throw another party, I'm sure."

"So you like him, then?" Avi asked.

It took me a second to remember that they didn't know this. I'd only told Lisa. This was a conversation I had meant to have up at the cabin—me "calling dibs" on Jeff. "I . . . yes. I do."

"I thought so. Do you think he likes you back?"

I thought about his mom calling me his girlfriend, letting me into his hospital room and not Lisa. I screwed the lid back onto my mascara and said, "I think so."

She smiled. "I'm glad for you. And him."

She squeezed my shoulder and I hoped that meant we were fine, that she was okay with Jeff and me in the future.

"Is everyone ready?" Morgan asked, pulling her final shirt selection over her head.

"As I'll ever be," I mumbled.

So far I had managed to maintain my calm. Even in Dallin's packed house. Beyond packed. There were so many people there that I guessed a lot of them weren't even from our school. I had apologized five point three times to Dallin's parents, who had now shut themselves in their bedroom to get away from the noise. I wished there was a bedroom for me to shut myself in.

Instead, I stood in the corner of the basement, a Dr Pepper in my hand, watching Lisa and Morgan talk to Wyatt and Sawyer by the pool table. This was my kind of fun—observing the party from the sidelines. I wished I had brought my camera.

Avi sidled up beside me. "You look bored," she said.

"No, I'm good. Just taking a breather."

"You should get out there and dance or something."

"I think I'm good right here," I said with a smirk.

"I'm bored too," she admitted. "Do you know who always made parties more fun?"

"Yes."

188

"Jeff," she answered anyway.

I laughed. "He did."

"Do you know what he did at the bonfire on the way up to the cabin?"

The bonfire that I missed because I was stuck in the library. "What?"

"He climbed a tree, in the dark, and scared us all."

"I thought you were in his car. Didn't you see him climb it?"

"No, we were trying to find dry wood to start a fire. And then when everyone got there, Jeff started making strange noises. We thought it was a bear or something. I think even Dallin was scared for a while."

I took a sip of my Dr Pepper. "I thought it started snowing right when you got there."

She pursed her lips to the side in thought. "It was probably like twenty minutes after we got there."

"Oh." I wouldn't let that hurt my feelings. With Jeff scaring people and the snow, it was understandable why they might not have noticed I wasn't there. "I didn't hear the rest of this story. What happened after that? After you left?"

"Well, Lisa said you probably went down with Jeff so we should go on without you. I wasn't sure why you would, but I kind of guessed, you know?"

I nodded.

"And then we drove up to the cabin. At like two o'clock in the morning your parents called Lisa asking if you were there. I guess that was right after the police found your stuff in Jeff's car. They were destroyed."

I looked at my feet. I didn't really need to imagine that part again.

"The roads were too icy to drive that night, but we left as soon as we could the next morning and spent the next two days searching the river for you." She grabbed my hand. "It was awful, Autumn."

"I'm so sorry."

"I know you didn't want this party but it really was a big deal for all of us. Dallin, Zach, Lisa, Morgan, Connor, and probably a bunch of these people that you don't even know were out there looking for you." My hurt feelings morphed into shame. She was right. I was moping in the corner, feeling sorry for myself that my amazing friends wanted to throw me a party, and half these people had been searching the river for me. I needed to find Dallin and tell him thank you.

Lisa stepped in front of us before I could move. "Two days in a row," she said.

"What?" I asked.

"This is like a record or something."

"What are you talking about?" Avi asked.

"Dax Miller."

190

"He's here?" Avi asked.

My heart dropped to my feet.

Lisa moved to the side and I immediately saw him across the room. It took me several deep breaths to realize he wasn't alone. A girl I didn't recognize, with choppy black hair, stood next to him. She was saying something to him and he was leaning close and nodding. His expression didn't seem hard like it had the last time he was talking to me.

Lisa lowered her voice as if he could somehow hear her from all the way across the room with the music at full blast. "I don't think I've ever seen Dax at a party. I wonder what he's doing here."

"Someone probably invited him." Who, though?

"Should I tell Dallin to put away any valuables?" Avi asked.

I gasped and shot her a look.

"What?" Avi asked. "He's been in juvie. Who knows what for."

I had nearly forgotten how people talked about Dax. It was just talk before I knew him, but now it felt like an attack. "I don't think he's ever stolen anything. I thought he was in juvie for beating up someone who totally deserved it."

"I heard he beat up some freshman kid for looking at him wrong," Lisa said.

"He did not."

Lisa nudged me with her elbow. "How do you know? Did you become a Dax expert in the library? Was there a Dax section?" She laughed a little, but when I didn't join her she stopped suddenly. "Wait . . . did you?"

"Sort of. I—" The music stopped right in the middle of a song, and silence took over the room.

Dallin ran down the stairs yelling, "Autumn! Autumn! Has anyone seen Autumn?"

Lisa took my arm and raised it up in the air. "She's over here."

Dread was slowly pouring down my body from the top of my head, filling in every space down to my toes. "What does he want?" I asked.

"Who knows? It's Dallin."

That's what worried me.

"It's time for your speech!" he said.

When he arrived in front of me, I said, "Dallin, you are awesome, and thank you for this party, seriously. But don't make me give a speech."

He smiled. "That was a good try, but everyone in the room needs to hear that." Zach was at his side and they muscled me onto their shoulders, the whole time calling out, "Speech! Speech! Speech!"

I gripped their shoulders, afraid I'd fall off backward if they turned too fast. What Avi had just told me circled in my mind. *Be grateful*, I told myself. *Don't be a baby. You can handle this. Don't think about it so much.* Just because my mind said it didn't mean my body listened. My heart immediately jumped into high gear. I needed to say something, anything, so they'd let me down. I swallowed the fire that was burning up my throat and said, "It's so great not to be dead." Everyone cheered. "You guys are the best! Now let's party!" Dallin and Zach bounced me up and down and someone turned the music back on. I closed my eyes. Then finally I felt the floor beneath my feet. I opened my eyes and pushed my way through bodies and hands until I made it upstairs and outside.

It was freezing, which meant there would only be a few others out there. I walked until I couldn't see anyone, to the very back of Dallin's property, behind a shed. I bent over because I thought I was going to be sick, but nothing happened. My forehead was slick with sweat and I wiped it away, then leaned up against the shed. This wasn't normal—this many episodes so close together. Normally my medicine kept me pretty level. I knew it was the extreme amount of stress I'd been under lately. Something had to give. I needed an outlet.

CHAPTER 26

• • • • • • •

After a while, I'd managed to calm my emotions. I was heading back to the house on somewhat shaky legs when I saw Dax standing on the deck, looking out over the yard.

I had to walk by him to go in the house, so I put on my best smile and said, "Hi. I didn't know you were coming."

"Me neither."

I looked around, saw several people from school pretending not to be listening to us. That would probably bother him since apparently he didn't want people to think he had friends. I gestured for him to follow me and he did. I led him down two hallways and opened the second door on the right. The laundry room. It was empty just like I'd hoped it would be. It was a little cramped, not a great place to escape when I needed an open space, but now it would work, when I just needed privacy. I closed the door behind us.

"Your friends don't know, do they?" he asked.

"That you were in the library with me? No, I never told them." I knew he thought I was going to tell the whole school, but I'd kept his secret.

"No. About your anxiety. They don't know, do they?"

"Oh." I looked at my palms. "No."

"Why not?"

"I don't want them to treat me different."

"Why not?" he asked.

I leaned back against the dryer. "Because I don't."

"Don't you? It would be way easier than that." He pointed at the door, and I knew he meant the scene downstairs, with me barely holding it together.

"No. I know how to manage it." At least I normally did. Lately I wasn't so sure.

He didn't seem convinced either, which meant I needed to change the subject. "So . . ." I tugged on the front of his flannel. "What are you doing here?"

"It was the only way out of the house tonight."

A hint of disappointment dampened my smile. "Right. Lots of rules at the group home?"

"So many. It would be your dream come true. Rules posted on every surface."

I smiled. "That does sound like perfect order."

He laughed, then looked at the closed door behind him.

"Is she going to get mad that you left her?"

"Who?" he asked.

"That girl you came with."

"Faye? No. But I'll have to show her my face soon. I'm sure she'll be making a report tonight."

"What do you mean? Faye makes reports?"

"She lives at the group home. Mr. Peterson trusts her. She wanted to come here tonight. I needed a change of scenery."

"Right."

"What about you? They're throwing a party, so your boyfriend must be doing better."

I sighed. "No, he's not. And he's not my boyfriend. Maybe he never will be. Maybe he'll get better and things won't go back to normal. Maybe he'll realize that he doesn't like me at all. That he wants to go live in Alaska or become a circus performer. Maybe he'll want to be free. Like you."

Dax didn't respond to anything I'd said, just thoughtfully

nodded. His relaxed attitude unwound my tension. I matched him breath for breath until my mind was clear again.

My phone buzzed in my pocket and I wondered if Lisa was looking for me. I pulled it out and read the text. It was from Jeff's mom.

Jeff opened his eyes.

My chest expanded with joy.

"What?" Dax asked.

People started yelling the news down the hallway outside our door. Dallin must've gotten the text too.

"Jeff?" Dax asked.

"Yes, he opened his eyes."

"That's great."

I clasped my hands together, and Dax's eyes caught on the hot pink bracelet on my wrist. With his long-sleeved shirt on, I couldn't tell if he was wearing his. I dropped my hands and said, "Yes, it is. Guess I'll be at the hospital again this week, finding out if he wants to be a circus performer or . . ." I almost finished that sentence with the words *my boyfriend* but for some reason I couldn't. Not with Dax staring at me like that.

He nodded. "I better go."

"Dax," I called just as he grabbed hold of the doorknob. He looked back at me.

Can I tell my friends we know each other? That we're

friends? Are you keeping me a secret for some reason? "I'll see you Monday," were the final words my chicken brain settled on.

He left and I leaned back against the dryer and groaned. The library had been so much less complicated. I straightened up, shook out my hands, and opened the door as well. I nearly ran over Dallin, who was walking down the hall.

"Hey," I said.

Dallin squinted his eyes and I wasn't sure if that meant he had seen Dax leave seconds before me or if he was just curious as to why I was exiting his laundry room. Either way he didn't comment on it, instead saying, "I've been looking for you. I thought you left."

Lisa appeared from behind him. "Me too."

"Here I am."

"Did you hear the news about Jeff?" he asked.

"Yes."

"Cool. We're all going to the hospital tomorrow."

"All of us?" I asked, spinning my finger in the air to circle his entire house.

"Well, no, not all of us. Just us. His close friends. You, Avi, Morgan, Zach, Connor."

"Me," Lisa said.

"Is he out of the ICU now?" If he was, I hadn't gotten that text.

"Nope. We're going to fill the waiting room with friend energy," Lisa said.

"You in?" Dallin asked.

"Yes. I'll be there."

CHAPTER 27

· · · · · · ·

We arrived at the hospital Sunday evening ready to take over the waiting room with our magic friend power.

"Dallin parked on that row," Lisa said, pointing two rows up from where I was turning in to find a spot.

"I saw an open space over here." I pulled in and turned off the car. "Are we about to overwhelm Mrs. Matson with seven of us showing up at the same time?"

She shrugged. "I hope not. But she's probably bored, don't you think? She sits in a waiting room all day."

"True."

When we climbed out of the car, the others were

walking toward us. Dallin was carrying a baseball bat.

"Are you planning to beat someone?" I asked.

"Jeff needs some inspiration. He has six weeks before our first game." Dallin swung the bat like a ball had just been pitched to him.

"You're giving him a visual timeline?" I asked.

"Yes, yes, I am." He poked me in the stomach with the end of his bat. "I know how Jeff works. It will be motivating."

Lisa stole the bat from him and carried it over her shoulder as we walked into the hospital. Like always, tension spread across my shoulders the second I was inside. Maybe it was the hospital smell. I couldn't wait until Jeff was out of here.

Mrs. Matson's hands went to her mouth when she saw us, letting out a small squeal. "You're here! You're all here."

"We got your text yesterday," Dallin said, "and just wanted to come congratulate you and leave a gift for Jeff."

He held out the bat. Much like when I had held out the flowers, she squished Dallin into a hug, the bat between them. "Thank you, thank you," she said. When she pulled back she laid the bat on the table with the various other items she had there. "I'll put this in his room when they move him downstairs."

"Are they moving him out of the ICU?" I asked.

201

"Maybe. Hopefully. He opened his eyes but still hasn't said anything, so we'll see." She smiled and grabbed my hand, holding it between both of hers. "Oh, Autumn, I'm so glad you're here. Let me go check and see if the nurse is done drawing blood, and you can come see him, hon. Maybe you'll be our good luck charm again." With that, she left me alone with six sets of eyes on me.

Dallin was the first to speak. "Wait. Have you actually *seen* him?"

Lisa put her arm around my shoulder. "Don't you know that Autumn is his cousin?"

"Since when?" Dallin asked.

"Since his mom declared it," she said.

"Why you?"

"Because he . . ." I couldn't finish that sentence out loud. Dallin was Jeff's best friend. His very best friend. If he was asking that question, maybe I didn't have as much reason to believe Jeff and I were a possibility as I thought. "I don't know. I'm sorry," I finished.

Morgan picked up the bat off the table and held it out to Dallin. "Maybe you need to smash your way in there."

I appreciated her effort to break the ice but it didn't work. Dallin was hurt; I could tell even though he tried to play it off otherwise. "Not a big deal. I guess it's good that one of us has talked to him." He sank into the nearest chair and spun an empty Coke bottle on the table in front of him. "Anyone up for a game of spin the bottle?"

Avi sat next to him. Lisa tightened her hold around my shoulders reassuringly.

I wasn't sure what to say. Apologizing again seemed pointless.

Mrs. Matson poked her head back into the waiting room. "Okay, Autumn, come with me."

I wished I could tell her to take Dallin instead but I knew she wouldn't, and her saying no would only make it worse. I followed after her. When we were alone I asked, "Has the doctor said anything else about his recovery?"

"Tests have come back strong. His brain activity is good. He seems to have feeling in his limbs. He just needs to talk to us now and we'll all feel better."

I know I'd feel a lot better. "Dallin really wants to see him. He misses him."

"I know he's been here a lot, and I love that boy to death, but I can't trust him to be calm in Jeff's room. He's too much of a jokester."

I smiled. Dallin would probably find that reason funny. "Wait . . . he's been here a lot?"

"Almost every day."

I was surprised we hadn't crossed paths, but that made more sense to me than the Dallin who had been putting on a face all week. He really was worried.

She opened the door for me and left me alone.

I slowly made my way over to him. The stitches on his head had been removed; angry red holes lined the bright pink line down his forehead.

"Hey, Jeff," I said, sitting in my least favorite chair in the world. "How's it going? How about waking up and talking so that you can be moved to the social wing. Isolation was never your strong suit." And I'd like it much better too, because then everyone else would get to see him and I wouldn't feel guilty for being the only one.

His eyes fluttered open, startling me, even though it wasn't a new development. It was very disconcerting to see him like that, awake and yet not, but I tried to work past my initial reaction and be strong.

"Can you hear me?" I asked.

He blinked very slowly, but I didn't know if that was an actual answer. I stood and put myself in his field of vision. His eyes were unfocused, almost glassy, but they were green and beautiful and I was so happy to see them open. I gently placed a hand on his arm. "Can you see me? Dallin said to say hi." His eyes slowly closed and didn't open again. I sat back down, my breath short, my heart beating double time. I only stayed for a few minutes after that, then let myself out of the room.

When I went back to report, the waiting room was empty except for Lisa and Mrs. Matson. My heart sank.

"Anything new?" Mrs. Matson asked.

"He opened his eyes for a little while, but that was it."

She smiled. "I thought he might for you."

I wasn't sure how to respond to that.

Lisa stood. "Let us know when he gets out of the ICU so we can see him," she said.

"I will."

"Thanks."

"Come back and see us soon, Autumn," Mrs. Matson said.

I nodded, then left with Lisa. When we were in the elevator I asked, "Where did everyone go?"

"They all had different excuses, but I think they had planned on just staying to say hi and then leaving."

I put my face in my hands. "Don't sugarcoat it. Was everyone mad at me or just Dallin?"

"Mainly Dallin, but he'll get over it. It's not your fault."

"I didn't think Mrs. Matson would do that with everyone there."

"Me neither."

"I feel terrible."

"Autumn, don't feel terrible. You're her hope right now. You were only trying to help. Don't let Dallin make you feel bad."

It was too late. I already did. The elevator dinged on the bottom floor and we got out.

There was something else that was bothering me too. "I guess Jeff didn't talk about me to Dallin?"

"Not all guys tell their best friends everything. I'd trust his mom more than Dallin," Lisa said. "And his mom acted like he talked about you all the time."

"You're right." But I couldn't shake the worry. If Dallin didn't know Jeff liked me, maybe he didn't.

CHAPTER 28

• • • • • • •

I had dropped Lisa off at home and was heading home
myself when I saw a café and made a sharp turn into the
parking lot. I was starving.

The girl inside was sweeping the floor.

"Are you closed?"

"No."

I'd originally thought about getting a sandwich, turkey-
avocado maybe, but as I walked toward the register I
noticed a lit glass case of bakery items. There wasn't
much, the leftovers at the end of a long day, but somehow there were still two cronuts on a tray. My body

seemed to let out a breath of relief just at the thought of them, at the memory they conjured. If the memory of a conversation with Dax could relax me so much, how well would an actual conversation work?

"Are you ready?" the girl asked, coming around the counter.

"Yes, I'll take those two."

She bagged them and I paid, then raced out to my car.

Dax's caregiver raised his eyebrows when he opened the door.

"You're back," he said.

"Yes. I am. I'm Autumn, by the way. I don't think I introduced myself last time."

"Hello, Autumn. I'm Mr. Peterson. I take it I'll be seeing a lot of you."

"Much to Dax's dismay, yes," I said with a smile.

He smiled back and opened the door wider. "Come in."

I silently cheered and followed after him.

The house was lived in but organized. A bench seat with hooks lined the wall to my right in the entry-way, coats and hats hanging off it, shoes underneath it. I wondered how many foster kids actually lived here. I wondered if any of those things were Dax's.

"Follow me."

We passed four or five doors before coming to the one on the end. It was half open and I could see a bunk bed on the far wall. Mr. Peterson knocked on the door.

A voice that wasn't Dax's said, "Yeah?"

Mr. Peterson pushed open the door. "Hello, Russell," he said. Then, "Dax, you have a visitor."

"Who?" His voice sounded from a part of the room I couldn't see.

Russell was staring at me with a half smile.

"Autumn," Mr. Peterson said.

I wasn't sure if Dax made a face or something but Russell said, "Might not want to voice many opinions; she's standing right there."

Dax appeared around the door, again looking neither surprised nor happy to see me. His eyes went to the bag of cronuts I held, then back up to my face.

"She can stay until eight thirty," Mr. Peterson said, then walked away.

"What?" Russell called after him. "Why don't they have to follow the rules?"

When Mr. Peterson didn't respond, Russell got up and followed after him with loud protests.

I inched my way into the room that Dax had not emerged from. It was small, just fitting the bunk bed and two desks. "What rules are we breaking?" I asked.

"Free time is over at eight o'clock on school nights."

"Oh." I looked at my phone. It was ten after eight. "You get a whole twenty minutes extra?"

"Yes, apparently you've charmed Mr. Peterson."

"It wasn't hard," I said behind my hand like I was sharing a secret. "I could teach you."

He smiled and it transformed his whole face.

Before Dax could question my being there, I said, "I brought you the cronut I promised. We never had them when we escaped the library."

"You didn't promise."

"Well, I told you about them, so it's only right I provide."

I walked with determination to his desk. He backed up several steps so I didn't run him over. Now we both stood by his desk and I set the bag on top of it, next to his book. "You're still reading *Hamlet*," I said.

"The never-ending book."

I picked it up and fanned through its pages. "I've never read it." The book naturally opened to where the envelope addressed to Susanna was stuck between two pages. He still hadn't mailed it. I met his eyes.

If I'd thought Dax had changed his private ways in the last week and was now suddenly, of his own choice, going to share with me what this letter was all about, I was wrong. He nodded his head toward the bag I'd set on his desk. "Are we actually going to eat them?"

I set the book down, opened the bag, and pulled out a cronut. "There she is. Heaven."

He took a step closer and my skin prickled to life. "It doesn't look life-changing."

"Do not speak ill of the cronut until you try it."

He accepted the challenge and took a bite.

"Pretty good," he said through his mouthful.

"Pretty good!? Pretty good? It's the best." I retrieved mine and ate it in four bites, then let out a happy sigh. "You'll never be able to eat another donut again."

"You've ruined me?"

"Yes."

I watched his hands as he finished his off. "You're still wearing it," I said quietly.

"What?"

"The bracelet." That had to mean something. He really did need me as a friend in his life. I held up my wrist and freed mine from beneath my jacket. "Me too."

"I've just been too lazy to find a pair of scissors."

Right. Dax carried a knife around in his boot. I didn't believe that for a second. But I did believe that he was too proud or private or something to admit he needed a friend.

When I looked up, he was staring at me. I met his stare, determined not to look away. That was easier said than done. His eyes were deep brown and so piercing they seemed to see right through me. I was right. There was something about being around him, someone who had seen me at my worst, that made me relax.

He let out a frustrated breath. "I'm leaving in six months. You shouldn't come back."

"I know. You don't want attachments," I said. I'd have to try something different with him if I wanted this friendship.

"I don't have any. I'm worried you might."

I let out a scoffing breath. "I don't have any attachments. You're just a good distraction for me. I need a distraction." This might work if I could control my facial expressions.

"Distraction."

"I've been at the hospital. That environment stresses me out—sick people, the pressure to miraculously heal someone. It would be nice to have someone outside of that circle to talk to, to hang out with. No expectations. No pressure. Zero commitment." And that was all true. Maybe that's why he seemed to believe me.

He nodded. We were close. Too close. I should've taken a step away but for the first time all week the tension in my shoulders and the back of my neck was gone, so I was going to stay where I was. Even if it meant Dax staring at me. Even if it meant smelling his familiar scent of laundry detergent and spice. Even if it meant feeling the heat from his body radiating against mine.

I grabbed the sides of his shirt, surprising myself with the action. He didn't step away, and the rest of the tension in my shoulders drained down my spine. He snaked one arm around my waist and pulled me into a hug, smashing me against him. The move shocked me and I gasped, but didn't pull away. Friends hugged, we could hug. The tightness in his shoulders seemed to lessen as we stood there as well.

I looked up at him. His face, only inches away, seemed just as calm as I now felt. He was moving toward me, smelling like sugar, when I blurted out, "But no kissing. Just friends."

"Friends?"

"No. Friends are attachments, right? So no, we're distractions. Distracted friends."

He stopped, his look amused. "Okay."

Why couldn't I stop talking? "And distracted friends don't kiss. Guys get attached when they kiss me."

A full smile took over his face now. "No kissing, then." His voice was low and scratchy and I wanted to immediately throw my rule out the window. The only rule I knew would protect me from the arrangement I had just made up.

"Rule number four."

He laughed a little. "Okay."

"Just a distraction," I said, straightening up and backing away from him. I smiled. "A really good one."

He grabbed hold of my wrist, keeping me from moving farther away. "Just a distraction?"

I nodded. "We can make rule number five 'No Attachments' if you're worried."

Dax smiled and pulled me close again.

Mr. Peterson was true to his word and kicked me out right at eight thirty with a loud throat clearing as he walked down the hall, then a quick knock and a "Free time over." I grabbed the empty bakery bag, crumpled it into a ball, and said, "Thanks. See you later."

I didn't look back. I didn't want to know if Dax regretted our new arrangement. It didn't matter. He needed a friend right now, whether he wanted to admit it or not. And so did I, someone to get my mind off everything when I was feeling stressed. But my real commitment, my focus, needed to be on Jeff and helping him recover. This would work out perfectly.

CHAPTER 29

· · · · · · ·

got to school a little early the next day and waited in the parking lot for Dallin to arrive. He always parked in the same place, in the back row, facing out. I watched him as he backed into the spot. He reached over to the passenger seat, grabbed his backpack, and stepped out of the car. I did too. I had to make things right with Dallin. Not only had he been Jeff's friend forever, but in the last several months, I'd felt like we had become friends too. I didn't like him being mad at me.

"Hey," I said, holding up my fist for a bump.

He just stared at it and I let my hand fall to my side.

He did manage a "Hi," though, as he continued to walk.

I fell into step beside him. "Dallin, I didn't ask to see him. I'm sorry. His mom told me you were her top choice of visitors but she was worried about the jokes you might play." There was nothing wrong with a little white lie in the face of hurt feelings, right?

"Nice," he said. Not the reaction I was hoping for.

"Are you upset that you haven't been able to see him or are you upset that I have?"

"Both."

"Why?"

"Because I don't think you're right for him. Jeff thought otherwise, so he asked me to try with you. And I have, I've been trying. I've been trying even harder since he's been in there, hoping he could somehow sense it, or at least the universe would take notice. But I still don't feel like you're right for him. You've been messing with his head for months now."

"Messing with his head?"

"It's true. You don't care. You're constantly disappearing. Running off. Making Jeff chase you. I threw a party for you and you disappeared. It's like you think you're too good for us."

My mouth dropped open in shock, no words coming to me at first. That's how my anxiety was perceived by my friends? They thought I thought I was too good for them? "No, I don't. At all. I have other issues, but I've never thought that. Never."

I needed to swallow my pride and explain more, tell him about my anxiety disorder, but it's like he didn't hear me because he kept going. "He's always looking for you, chasing after you. Sneaking off with you. Just like he did at the bonfire."

"I wasn't at the bonfire. I never showed up. You guys left me in the library."

"But if you didn't have a history of disappearing . . ."

"He still would've left. Like you all did."

"But after you were discovered at the library and I found out you hadn't been at the bonfire, I realized he was chasing after you. And if he hadn't been, he wouldn't have been in such a big hurry. He would've been more careful."

My heart seemed to stop in my chest. "You think him being in the hospital is my fault?"

"I'm just saying . . ."

I stopped walking, my eyes stinging. He pivoted slightly, gave me a shoulder shrug, and kept walking. I stood there in the middle of the parking lot watching him go.

It took me a couple of minutes to decide if I was going to stay at school or get back in my car, drive home, and crawl into bed. At home I would dwell on Dallin's words all day long. They would circle around and around in my brain. I needed to talk to Lisa, to Avi and Morgan. Make sure Dallin was the only one who felt this way.

But in the meantime, I needed a distraction. Someone who I didn't have to talk about this problem with. Someone who I knew for sure didn't feel this way about me.

I found him by the buses with ten minutes to spare before school started. "Dax," I called out to him.

He nodded.

"Hey, can we talk? Can I talk to you?" I asked, breathless.

"Uh . . ." He looked at the students surrounding us.

I looked around as well, for somewhere more private if that's what he needed. The greenhouse was the closest building, rarely used in the winter. Without another word I headed there and hoped he'd follow. I also hoped it was unlocked. It was and he did. I stepped inside.

It was warmer, the air humid and smelling of soil. Rows of black planter boxes filled with mostly yellowing plants lined the tables.

"Tell me something happy," I said, turning to face him.

"Did you mistake me for someone else?"

That sentence alone lightened my mood. "I've had a crappy morning."

"But it's only seven thirty."

"I know."

He moved a planter box and sat down on the table. "What happened?"

"Stupid stuff. I don't want to talk about it. I need to get my mind off it."

He pointed at himself. "With your distraction?"

"Exactly."

He smiled and leaned back on his palms. When he was like this, unguarded and open, he was so cute. Okay, even when he was intense and closed off he was cute.

"What?" he asked.

I realized I was smiling too. "I want to take out my camera." My hand clutched the strap of my camera bag.

"Why?"

"Because you are very photographable." Dax surrounded by dead plants, the sun shining muted through the fogged up window behind him.

He raised his eyebrows.

"It's true."

"Not sure I should be flattered when I saw you taking a picture of a spider a few weeks ago."

"How do you know what I was taking pictures of a few weeks ago?"

"I walked right by you. Your vision is limited behind that camera."

I hadn't seen him at all. My vision *was* limited behind the camera, focused, uncluttered. That was one of the reasons I liked it. "It wasn't a spider. It was its web. It was frozen. And amazing. I'll have to show you how those turned out one of these days." I stopped. "Like, any day. You should come over to my house. My parents would probably love it."

"Your parents . . . they sent me a letter."

I laughed. I had forgotten about that letter. "They did. You're their hero."

"I thought I was yours."

I laughed again. "Yes. You are."

"You sound almost as sarcastic as I imagined you sounded when I read it."

"I was mad at you when I wrote it."

He seemed amused by this thought. "Why?"

"You didn't want to see me."

"You like to assume."

My heart did a somersault and I scolded it for that reaction. We'd established a rule. He didn't want an attachment and neither did I.

The bell rang, sounding through the campus. I looked up but then back at him, not moving.

"So, anyway, you need to drive over to my house and . . . Wait, can you drive?" I asked suddenly.

"I drove my mom's car from the end of the street to

the driveway when I was thirteen."

"Wow. That's impressive."

"I hit two mailboxes."

"Or not. So that's why you didn't want to borrow my car."

He smiled. "That is one of many reasons."

"I'm going to teach you how to drive it. You would love the freedom it gives you." I felt bad that nobody in his life had ever taught him how to drive, and looking forward, I couldn't see that changing. It was a life skill he needed if he wanted to be as free as he claimed he did.

He was still sitting, leaning back on his palms. "That does not sound like one of your better ideas."

"It is an excellent idea."

He brushed some dirt off his palms. "Don't you have to go?"

"Don't *you* have to go?"

"I could stay here all day," he said.

"I could too," I countered.

His smile took over his face. "Really?"

"Oh you think you know me so well now, huh? You think being late to class would bother me?"

"Yes. You'd hate to make your teacher mad at you."

I narrowed my eyes at him, but then said, "You're right. I have to go." I rushed toward the door, but when I was almost there, I circled back around and threw my arms around him. "You did your job perfectly. Thank you."

He chuckled and put his arms around me. Since he was up on the table, my head fit just below his chin. I closed my eyes and sighed. I went to pull away but he held on. At first I thought maybe he needed a longer hug but when his body shook with silent laughter I knew he was doing it to bug me.

"The late bell is going to ring," I said.

"I know."

"Let me go, brat."

He did and I ran out the door, throwing him a smile over my shoulder as I did. He still hadn't moved to leave, but a lazy smile was on his face.

Just a distraction, I reminded myself as I ran to class.

CHAPTER 30

had tried to justify going home at lunch so I didn't have to face my friends, but that would only make Dallin's statement about me seem true. I clutched my brown lunch sack in my fist and stepped into the cafeteria. The wall of noise hit me first, then the competing food smells—today it was mostly spaghetti and garlic. I kept my focus and headed for our table.

Lisa smiled and slid down the bench to make room for me. It wasn't until I was seated and took in all the other smiling, talking faces that I realized Dallin wasn't there. A scan of the room didn't locate him either.

"Where's Dallin?" I asked Lisa.

"Not sure."

So he was the one running away now? I cleared my throat. "I'm sorry that I was the only one who got to see Jeff last night," I said to the table.

Avi patted my arm. "I'm not mad. You're the one who might actually make a difference. You like each other. I hear emotions can play a big part in healing."

The rest of the group chimed in with various versions of how they weren't mad at me either.

"Autumn, the miracle worker," Lisa said quietly from beside me with a smile.

I wasn't sure if she was talking about healing Jeff, or smoothing things over with my friends. Either way, "I still have some work to do."

Lisa took out one of her Oreos and handed it to me, then, as if she knew I was saying all this because of Dallin, she said, "Dallin is an idiot."

I smiled and took a bite, glad to know she was on my side . . . if there were sides. There weren't sides. I was going to fix this.

"He's out of the ICU?" I hugged Mrs. Matson. I couldn't believe how happy I was to be on a different floor. With different chairs and a different television in the corner.

"Yes." She was beaming with excitement.

"Did you text Dallin?" I had gotten the text after school and waited a full hour before I came because I wanted him to be able to come first.

"Yes, but I think he has baseball practice or something."

"Oh. Right." Crap. Were they already starting that? It seemed so early. Must've been preseason. "So is Jeff talking yet?"

"He's a lot more aware but still sleeping most of the time. The doctors are slowly weaning him off his pain medication. They think that might be part of the reason he's not fully awake. Come. He needs to see you."

His room was smaller but with fewer machines. And he had a window this time that overlooked the parking lot. I sat down next to him and took his hand. "Hey, Jeff. We miss you. I need you to get better. Maybe you can talk to Dallin and tell him I'm a decent human being. He seems to think otherwise right now. That's a good reason to talk, yes? For my benefit."

Another good reason to talk was so I stopped telling so many bad jokes. That would be for his benefit, of course. If he'd heard any of them, that is.

He let out a small groan and my heart jumped.

"Jeff?"

He rolled his head to the side and his eyes fluttered open. His mom had said he'd been awake more but I hadn't anticipated how much clearer his eyes would look. Like he could actually see me. Joy rushed through me.

"Hi," I said softly.

A smile played on his lips.

"Your mom would be really happy if you talked. Seeing your gorgeous green eyes is enough for most of us, but not for her, apparently."

He squeezed my hand and then closed those eyes. I waited, hoping maybe he just needed to rest for a minute, but he didn't open them again.

I was feeling pretty good about this report I'd be able to give to Mrs. Matson, until I arrived at the waiting room and saw Dallin there waiting to talk to her as well. She was having a discussion with the doctor.

"You had to be first," Dallin said under his breath to me when I joined him.

"I tried to wait. I didn't realize baseball practice had started."

Mrs. Matson came over to us. "So the doctor still thinks it's important that he not have a lot of activity in his room for the next little while. I want all of you to be able to see him, but we're going to have to keep it to a minimum. One extra guest a day."

"Dallin can still see him today, though, right?" I asked in a panic.

"Yes, of course. But can you work it out with your

friends so that he doesn't get overwhelmed with visitors?"

"Yes," I said, then bit my lip. "I mean, yes, Dallin can create a schedule."

"Will you, Dallin?" Mrs. Matson asked.

"Yes," he said shortly.

"I better go," I said. Mrs. Matson didn't need my report. Nothing new had happened. "Have a good visit."

Dallin only nodded. I had wanted to fix this, but somehow I'd made it even worse.

CHAPTER 31

• • • • • • •

Mr. Peterson must've told him who was waiting, because Dax came out to the porch prepared to leave—shoes, jeans, and jacket on. He shut the door behind him and headed to my car with just a "Hey."

"Hi," I said, catching up to him.

When we were both in my car, I turned to him. "Bad day?"

"Better now."

I gripped the wheel, not wanting to see the expression that went along with those words. We both still needed to be unattached. Seeing Jeff today had reaffirmed the fact that he was going to get better and everything was going to go back to how it was supposed to be.

I wasn't sure where I was driving until I ended up in front of the library. Dax seemed surprised with my choice too.

"You have homework to do?" he asked.

"I have shoes to retrieve."

"Still?"

"It hasn't been that long." I pulled into the underground lot.

We walked toward the door together. The first hall we came to was empty, and that brought back the feelings of the first few hours in the library. But when we made it to the main hall, several other people were roaming about, which made things better, different.

"You good?" he asked.

I nodded. We walked through the glass hallway and downstairs to the main library. I checked under the chair first, hoping I didn't have to ask anyone. They weren't there. I lingered as I remembered Dax reading in that chair, remembered where we'd shared the sleeping bag right below it. I wondered if Dax was remembering the same thing. We caught each other's eyes.

"We should go see if there are any apples to steal in the kitchen," I whispered.

He smiled.

I took a deep breath and walked to the checkout desk. The lady behind it waited for me to speak.

"I left a pair of black boots here. Did they get turned in?"

"Black boots . . ." She searched beneath the counter and came up with my boots, setting them on top.

"So this is what an ankle wedge looks like," Dax said quietly beside me.

The lady gave me a hard look. "You must be the girl who was stuck here last weekend."

I wasn't prepared for her to call me out on it. I nodded.

"Your mom has given us a list of new closing procedures."

How did I respond to that? Was she mad at me?

"Probably a good thing," Dax said, swiping my boots and leading us away.

I couldn't believe my mom had done that. Okay, actually I could believe it. It was in her nature, but I was so embarrassed.

Before we got up the stairs and to the glass hallway again Dax said, "Who cares what she thinks? She's nobody. Don't worry about it."

I don't know if he thought I couldn't handle stairs at that moment or what, but he led me to the elevator and pushed the button.

"I don't care," I assured him. I really was fine.

The light dinged and the doors opened. We climbed inside. Just as he was about to push the button for the bottom floor, I pushed the one for the top and the doors slid shut.

He was still holding my boots so I took them from him, clutching them to my chest. "Have you ever seen the bell tower?" I asked.

"No. I haven't."

"You should."

Considering it only had to go up two floors, the elevator took forever. When the doors finally opened, we stepped out. I wondered if the door to the tower would still be unlocked or if we'd have to turn around and go back down. I pushed on the bar and it opened with a loud creak. It was dark this time, and I took out my phone and turned on the flashlight. The stairs up to the top didn't look or feel any more sturdy than they had the last time I climbed them. And now, with the two of us on them, I laughed nervously with each step.

We made it to the top and I opened the door. I took in a deep breath of cool air. The wooden owl on the railing looked at us as we both sat down in the small space that overlooked the peaked roofline. We were knee to knee, the space was so small.

"Cool, right?" I turned off the flashlight on my phone, the streetlights outside enough to dimly light the area.

"Yes. I'm surprised I haven't seen this before. Our stay wasn't my first stint in the library."

"You don't say," I said, feigning surprise.

He smiled, then looked up. "You rang this bell one night, didn't you?"

"Nobody heard it."

"I did. I wasn't sure what it was."

"It was me."

Sitting there, I realized this tower was probably off-limits for guests. If we got caught we'd get in trouble.

"Anyway, I wanted to show you. We should go."

"Because you're worried, or because you have somewhere you need to be?"

"The first."

"You worry too much."

"I know. It's kind of my thing."

My arms rested across my knees, which were pulled up to my chest. He ran a slow finger across my forearm. I closed my eyes, letting all the tension of the day, of coming back to the library, pour out of me.

"I'm trying to manage things. It's been hard. It will get better when things are back to normal. There's just a lot of stuff going on right now."

Dax reached up and held on to the railing behind him, seeming to consider this. "What happened this morning before school?"

I sighed, not wanting to go there. Just the thought of what Dallin had said made me shudder. "Nothing."

"You're not going to tell me?"

I held up a fist. "I'll play you for it."

"Play me for it?"

"Rock, paper, scissors. Winner gets a secret." I was willing to risk that for the chance at asking him a question. I had a couple I really wanted answered.

He smiled. "Okay."

"Best two out of three?" I asked.

"Sure."

He won the first hand with a rock that crushed my scissors. I growled, then got ready again. The second hand I went with paper, and he did a rock again. Now it was a tie. I looked at him. He'd done two rocks in a row. Would he do it a third time? He gave me a calm stare, not giving anything away. Dax was unpredictable, so he'd go with something different. Although, more unpredictable would be if he did the same for a third time.

"One, two, three," I said and held out a paper. He was holding a rock again. "Ha! I won."

"You did," he said, seeming impressed.

"Who knew you were so bad at this game?"

"Have you been practicing smack talk?"

"Only because you keep losing. I'm getting plenty of practice."

He smirked and grabbed hold of the rail over his head again. "What's your question?"

My eyes went to his left arm. His tattoo. Tattoo or Susanna? Tattoo or Susanna? "Why haven't you sent that letter in your book to Susanna?" I asked.

His smile fell. "Because . . ." He put his hands through his hair. "Ugh. You're a horrible person, you know that?" He said it with a smile so I just nodded.

"Yes, I am."

He held his hand forward, palm up. "You see this?"

My eyes went to his tattoo. "Yes."

"This was our very last court date. My mom had had months to change. Went through three different drug rehab programs, six court dates, two hospitalizations. And as we sat there in court, me on one side, her on the other, the judge asked her if she was choosing meth over her son. She was. It's the last time I ever spoke to her."

"She lost her rights to you that day?"

He gave a short nod.

"I'm sorry, Dax."

"I already told you, it was the day I finally let go. I'm free."

I didn't believe him any more today than I had the first time he'd said it. Everyone needs someone they can count on. "And the letter?"

"Is everything I still need her to answer."

"Susanna is your mother?"

"Yes."

"So why can't you send it?"

"Because she'll think I'm trying to reconnect, and I'm not."

"What are you trying to do?"

"Get basic information that kids with parents have about themselves."

"Why do you care what she'll think, then?"

"I don't."

"Then send it."

"I will." He looked up at me through his lashes. "And you just got way too much information for that win."

I had so many follow-up questions, but I let them go for now. Despite the fact that he looked completely calm, I understood how emotionally draining talking about things like that could be. "I totally did."

"Are you going to make me win my question now?"

I fake sighed. "I guess not. Since technically you answered two. What was your question again?"

"This morning . . . ?"

"Oh right. This morning . . ." Spit it out, Autumn. He just told you what happened on the worst day of his life; you can tell him this. "Dallin told me that I was the reason Jeff was in the hospital."

"Who's Dallin?" he asked, his eyes hardening.

"Jeff's best friend."

"And why would he think something so idiotic?"

"Because I'm always leaving or finding a place to hide or going into a corner at parties, and he said that Jeff always felt the need to go running after me. And he was doing that again when he crashed into the river—running after me. Dallin basically hates me now."

"Then you told him about your anxiety?"

"No. I didn't want to use it as a defense. To make it seem like I was making excuses. And I really don't want them to treat me differently."

"That's a stupid argument."

"Thanks."

"You told *me*."

"But my friends aren't you."

"What does that mean?"

"You've . . . you've seen things they haven't. I'm worried they won't understand."

"Maybe you should trust them."

"But I have no idea how they'll react."

He nodded slowly.

"What?"

"You mean you can't control how they'll react. You're worried they won't like you."

I picked a flaky piece of paint off the rail by my head. "Yeah."

"You need to tell them."

"I will when you send your letter."

He gave a short nod. "Well played."

The breeze coming in from the still-open door picked up and I shivered.

"My ears are cold," I said.

One side of his mouth lifted into a half smile, but he didn't move.

I used the rail to pull myself to standing. "Let's go."

He stood as well, and as I turned on my flashlight and shifted to head down the stairs he stepped in front of me. I took a surprised gasp. He put his hands over my ears. They were warm. "I don't mind being your distraction, but I won't always be here."

"I know." And he was right. I needed to let my friends in and make sure I could work through things on my own before he really did disappear. I needed to make sure I no longer needed a distraction.

CHAPTER 32

• • • • • • •

Between the hospital and library visit I had been gone way longer than I told my parents I would be. I opened the front door, carrying my boots under my arm, and shut it as quietly as possible, hoping that if I just snuck into my room they'd think I'd been here the whole time. But when I turned around my brother was standing in the hall, leaning against the wall, staring at me.

"Owen!" I squealed. "What are you doing here?"

"Wednesday classes got canceled, and since I only have Monday, Wednesday, Friday classes, I thought I'd take Friday off and make a week of it."

"It must be nice to be in college, playing by your own rules, being your own boss." I smirked at him.

"Looks like someone else I know is her own boss too. What's up with being gone all night?"

I rolled my eyes. "It's only nine. And I was just saving the world, one coma patient at a time."

He scrunched up his face. "Sorry. Is he still not doing well?"

"Actually Dax is doing much better."

"Who's Dax?"

"Dax? Did I say Dax?"

Owen raised his eyebrows and nodded his head.

"I meant Jeff. He got out of the ICU today. The doctors say things are looking good. So hopefully things are only going to get better from here." I was rambling, so I stopped.

"That's good about Jeff. Now who's Dax?"

My cheeks went hot.

"Wow," Owen said.

"No, it's nothing. He's a friend."

"Ha. That's not what it looks like. I want to meet this *friend*."

I shoved his arm. "Don't be such a brother."

I started to escape down the hall when he stopped me with, "Why are you carrying shoes?"

"These got left in the library. I picked them up today."

"First time back?"

"Yep."

"And you handled it okay?"

"Why wouldn't I?"

"Oh, I don't know, last time you were in the library you fainted with a panic attack."

"I handled it." With help.

He gestured toward the kitchen. "Just a heads-up: Mom was worried about your emotions and stuff visiting the hospital so much." And this was another reason I had a hard time telling my friends—I already had enough people worried about my emotions.

"Look at you, home fifteen minutes and already playing my spy."

He looked at his watch. "I've actually been home for two hours. You haven't been."

"Details, details." I finished my walk down the hall toward my room.

He called after me. "You owe me some quality sibling time this week. No acting like I'm not here."

"I'll pick out the nail polish color tomorrow."

"Hey now. I pick out my own nail polish," he said. I smiled and closed the door behind me, then sank to the floor. I felt a headache forming behind my eyes. I hoped I could go to sleep fast tonight, not play and replay the day in my head for hours like my brain sometimes liked to do.

★ ★ ★

Dallin stood at the head of the lunch table the next day like he was conducting a meeting. I had a lingering headache from the day before, and this looked like it was only going to make it worse.

He pounded on the table with his fist to get our attention. "Jeff got out of the ICU yesterday, but his mom requested only one visitor a day. I'm sending you all a text right now with the schedule for the next seven days. If you can't do the day I assigned you, try to find someone to switch with." Serious-Dallin was tripping me out. I wasn't used to him.

My phone buzzed with his incoming text. I pulled up the schedule.

Today—Connor.

Wednesday—Avi.

Thursday—Zach.

Friday—Dallin.

Saturday—Lisa.

Sunday—Morgan.

Monday—Autumn.

Repeat until the Jeff is Free party that I will host when Jeff is free.

Seriously? He was going to play this game? It was obvious he was still mad at me. The rest of the group was busy talking and switching days. I looked up at Dallin. He played innocent.

Lisa leaned over to me. "I'll switch with you."

"But you haven't seen him yet."

"It's okay. He'd rather see you."

"I don't know that he knows who he's seeing. It's fine." I could handle this if it would make Dallin feel better.

"Maybe he'll start doing better and his mom will allow more visitors."

I nodded. "Hopefully."

When the bell rang and everyone had cleaned up their stuff, Dallin lingered behind until we were the only two left. "It's only fair, Autumn," he said. "Since you've already seen him a lot."

"I agree. Good job," I said. It was obvious he wanted me to get mad at him, but I was determined to mend our friendship.

Just because I couldn't see Jeff, didn't mean I wasn't going to get a report. I needed that for my mental health. So the next morning, I found Connor before first period. He was at his locker, shoving more papers into an already paper-filled mess. "How was he?"

"What? Who?"

"Jeff. You saw him yesterday, right? How was Jeff?"

"Oh. Hi, Autumn. Nice to see you this morning too."

I smiled. "Hi, Connor. How has your morning been so far?"

"It was good. I overslept, I—"

I smacked his arm. "Connor. Come on."

He laughed. "He was fine. Really tired, but he looked good. The doctor said he should be more and more alert every day."

"That's good. So good." Six more days until I could see him for myself. I could handle six more days.

I held my camera up to my eye and twisted the outside ring back and forth, making Owen go from blurry to clear over and over again.

"You're not taking my picture, are you?" he asked from his spot on the couch next to me.

"Don't worry, diva. I know you like to do your hair first."

He pointed the remote at the television and clicked it off. "Actually, not for your pictures. You have a way of capturing things that looks good every time."

I was caught off guard by the compliment. "Thanks."

"I'm serious. Is that what you're thinking for college? Photography?"

"No. Not at all. It's too . . ."

"Risky?"

"Yes."

"And what's wrong with risk? What's wrong with going after the uncertain choice? The one you haven't planned to a T."

"You know what's wrong with that. It would stress

me out too much. I need security."

He reached out for my camera and I handed it to him. He put it up to his eye and took a picture, then looked at the result on the screen with a sour face. "All I'm saying is you have talent."

"You're my favorite brother."

"Always."

I collected my camera back from him.

"I thought you'd be at the hospital today," he said.

I groaned, trying not to think about it. "Today is Avi's day."

CHAPTER 33

• • • • • • •

"Jeff talked to you?" I asked, still not believing it. Why wasn't Avi jumping up and down like I wanted to? Why hadn't she called us all last night? "This is amazing news!" Relief poured through me.

Avi opened her bag of chips, then shrugged. "Has he not done that before?"

The four of us—Lisa, Morgan, Avi, and I—were sitting together in the cafeteria. The boys were at some baseball lunch meeting. I had stopped eating the moment she shared the news.

"What did he say?"

"Not much. Just hi and asked how long he'd been there."

I tried to control the tiny bit of jealousy that Jeff had talked to Avi first, that I had missed it, and focus on the huge amount of joy that he had talked at all. "Did you tell his mom?"

"Was I supposed to?"

"No, it's fine. I'm sure she knows. Whose turn is it today?" Instead of waiting for an answer, I pulled out my phone and referred to Dallin's text.

"Zach's," Morgan said at the same time I read it.

"You think Zach will switch with me?" I asked.

"Probably not," Avi said.

I groaned. Why had I turned over the scheduling power to Dallin in the hospital? I was trying to be nice, but it hadn't made a difference.

Lisa squeezed my arm. "Do you want me to talk to Dallin?" All my friends thought Dallin was being unreasonable too.

"No." Because if I were being honest, there was still a bit of fear in me that Jeff really didn't care about seeing me. We weren't together, we never had been. What made me think I was so special?

I had passed Dax in the hall after lunch and slipped him a note. A note that had told him to meet me between sixth and seventh period where I now stood—behind the cafeteria. I hadn't anticipated the Dumpsters and the stench they'd be emitting.

Dax rounded the corner, his stride slow and confident. He looked at the trash when he got to me and raised his eyebrows.

"I was hoping you could help me find my retainer. I think it got thrown away."

The pleasant look dropped off his face. "Really?"

I laughed. "No."

He smiled.

I grabbed onto the lapels of his jacket and pulled him a little closer to me.

"Hi," he said in a low voice.

"Hi," I sighed.

"Do you even wear a retainer?" he asked.

I flashed a wider smile. "Only at night. What about you? Did you ever have braces?"

"That wasn't exactly top priority for any of my foster parents."

"Well, then you got lucky, because you have very pretty teeth."

He shrugged. "You haven't looked close enough, then."

I tilted my head and he gave me a fake smile that made me laugh. His front two teeth overlapped a little and his bottom ones were a bit more crooked, but they weren't distracting at all. "I was right, very pretty."

He took a fistful of either side of my sweater at my waist and said, "You're not a very good liar."

His hold made me feel light on my feet, like I wasn't quite touching the ground. I braced myself with my palms against his chest. "Then you must not be good at reading me anymore because I'm not lying. I, on the other hand, am excellent at reading you. Just like in that game of rock, paper, scissors we played. Read you like a book."

He laughed. "I'll work on my poker face."

"You should come over today after school."

"To your house?"

"Yes, my brother is in town. I think you'd like him."

"I don't like anyone, remember?"

I took another small step forward. "I don't think that's true."

"I do like distractions," he said.

"Me too." It was obvious he didn't want to meet my brother, probably thought that meant commitment or something. "Okay, fine, there's a park by my house. You have my address? It was on that letter my parents sent you.

He nodded.

"Meet me at the park? Four o'clock?"

"I will try."

"Try hard."

He smiled, and I could read his face. It said he wasn't coming. I pretended not to notice. I wasn't going to give him an easy way out. If he didn't want to come, he'd have to not come knowing I was sitting in the cold, waiting for him.

Dax and I headed back around the cafeteria and through the main doors together. I said, "Bye," and he gave me a head nod as we split to go separate ways. That's when I saw Lisa leaning against a locker, staring at me. I smiled.

She dragged me by the arm into the closest bathroom and said, "Spill. Now."

"Spill what?"

"You know what. I saw you pass him a note after lunch. How do you know him?"

I checked under each stall to make sure they were empty. "He was in the library with me." There was no use in keeping it a secret anymore.

"Dax?"

"Yes."

"Dax Miller?"

"Yes," I said with more emphasis.

Her brow wrinkled in confusion. "He was in . . . wait . . . he was in the library with you? All weekend?

As in trapped? As in you weren't alone?"

"We were trapped together."

"NO WAY!"

"Yes . . . way."

"Why didn't you tell me?"

"I'm sorry. He swore me to secrecy. Long story. Not one for the bathroom."

"You'll tell me all the details later?"

"Yes."

"Was he . . . ?" She searched for a word to finish that sentence.

"He was nice, fun."

"Fun?"

"Okay, not like Jeff fun. He was a little cold at first, standoffish. But once we'd been there for a while he was . . . fun."

"That's so crazy. You know Dax Miller now. Nobody knows Dax Miller." She paced in front of the sinks. "You know Dax Miller." She stopped with a gasp. "Wait. Do you *know* know Dax Miller? Have you guys like . . . ?"

"No."

She smiled. "Huh. He'd be a good kisser, don't you think? Those lips, those eyes."

I shoved her arm. "Stop." I could not think about kissing him. I'd already banned myself from doing that.

She studied my face and I knew my cheeks were red.

"You like him," she whispered.

"No. I don't. He doesn't like anyone, and he's not boyfriend material. At all."

She didn't seem to believe me because she said, "Autumn, what about Jeff? He needs you right now. He's still recovering, then he's going to have physical therapy and have to get back into life, and negative emotions might have a bad effect on him."

My jaw tightened. "I know. I'm not going anywhere. There is nothing between me and Dax."

"Then why are you hanging out with him?"

"He's just a distraction."

"Television is a distraction. Dax is a hostile takeover."

"He hasn't taken over anything." Nothing at all. He wanted to be gone as soon as possible—no attachments—and I had just needed something to keep my mind occupied. Things would be back to normal soon.

CHAPTER 34

• • • • • • •

I got a text during seventh period from Mrs. Matson.

Jeff asked about you. Can you come after school today?

Jeff asked about me. Jeff was awake enough to talk and he asked about *me*. This was great news . . . really great news, I told myself again.

I texted her back.

Yes! Of course.

It was all my brain could think about the rest of school. I went immediately to the hospital after school for two reasons. One, so my parents, who were concerned about my emotional state (thank you for the heads-up,

Owen), wouldn't tell me I couldn't go. And two, so that I wouldn't interfere with Zach's time. He wouldn't head over until after baseball practice.

By the time I got to Salt Lake the anticipation of see-ing Jeff, of *talking* to Jeff, had me so jittery that my hands were shaking. At first I sat in the car, trying to calm my nerves, but realized that it was only making me more anxious. I rushed through the parking lot and straight to the waiting room.

Mrs. Matson's smile was brighter than ever. "Autumn, we've missed you. You haven't been visiting."

"We've been on the one-visitor-a-day schedule. Like you said."

"That was meant for his friends. You're family, remember?" She gave me a wink.

"Oh. Right." Dallin would die if he'd heard that.

"Come on. Jeff's waiting for you." She tucked my arm in hers and led me to him.

When we walked in, he was asleep. My heart sank. But his mom left me at the foot of his bed and went to his side. She patted his arm. "Honey, you have a visitor."

He groaned and his eyes fluttered open. "Mom?" It was so good to hear his voice again after two weeks.

"Yes. Hi."

"Can I get some pain meds?"

"I know you're sore, but not yet."

"No respect," he said, and a small smile flitted across his lips.

I smiled too. It was the first sign I'd seen of Jeff being Jeff and that made me know everything was going to be okay.

"In a couple hours. You're doing good. Down to twice a day."

He nodded.

"Autumn is here."

"Hi," I said, and his eyes were immediately on me.

"Mom. That's the kind of thing you lead with," he said. "Now she thinks I'm an addict."

"She doesn't think you're an addict."

"No, I do," I said.

He tried to laugh but it came out as a cough.

"Come and sit," he said, pointing to the chair.

"Are you sure? You seem tired."

"I'm bored. And since I can't have pain meds . . ."

His mom squeezed my arm on her way toward the door. "Not too long. He really does need his rest," she said in a low voice.

"I didn't lose my hearing, Mom," he said.

Mrs. Matson sighed and shook her head, but there was so much joy in her eyes.

I lowered myself to the chair by his bed. "How are you?"

"Pretty good. Did you see my cool new scar?"

My eyes went to his forehead and the pink line there that would forever remind him of this accident. "I did. I spent several days checking it out."

"I heard you've been here. Thank you."

"Of course."

He may have thought he could handle a long conversation but his speech was thick and eyes were already becoming lidded.

"You need to sleep."

"No, I'm fine. Tell me everything I missed in the last couple weeks."

"Not much. A basketball game. A party." *Dallin accusing me of putting you in the hospital.*

"Sounds fun." His blinks were becoming slower, longer.

"You're going to fall asleep on me."

"I am," he said. "I'm sorry."

"Please don't be. I'll come back."

"Come tomorrow."

"Tomorrow is Dallin's day." The only day I didn't want to risk showing my face here.

He reached for my hand and I provided it for him. "Come tomorrow," he said like he hadn't heard me.

"Okay."

"Promise?"

"I promise."

He nodded, but his eyes were already closed.

I left the hospital room with a smile. Jeff was awake. My life was now back on my previously planned course.

CHAPTER 35

· · · · · · ·

was stuck in traffic outside of Salt Lake. It was only
3:45. I thought I'd miss after-work traffic, but it was
going to turn my forty-five-minute drive into an hour
for sure. I rubbed my neck. That's when I remembered
Dax and the meeting I'd set up with him. Four o'clock at
the park by my house. I'd totally forgotten with the news
about Jeff wanting to talk to me. Why didn't Dax have
a working phone I could call? I was a horrible person.

No, it would be fine.

Dax wouldn't be there. I'd seen that in his eyes earlier. He wasn't going to come. How would he get there

anyway, even if he had wanted to? He had no car and didn't know how to drive.

My dashboard clock said five thirty by the time I made it to my neighborhood. It turned out the traffic wasn't work related at all; there'd been a big accident. I'd called my parents and let them know where I was and that I'd be later than I thought.

I slowed down as I drove by the park, just to make sure. At first I thought I was right and relaxed back into my seat, but then I saw a lone figure in a dark coat sitting on a bench by the swings. I gasped and pulled against the curb, shutting off my engine. He came?

The park was empty as I walked toward him—too late for the kids who normally occupied it. Dax was reading, lit by the glow of the streetlamp, and an image of him in the library came back to me so strongly that I had to stop for a moment. I shook it off.

"I'm so sorry," I said.

He looked up, his dark eyes meeting mine. He didn't seem upset. "Hey."

"How did you get here?"

"Like how did I come to exist or . . . ?"

"Funny." I sat down next to him on the bench and he closed his book—still *Hamlet*—and set it beside him. "Did someone bring you?"

"I took the bus."

"You took the bus for me?"

"I take the bus for everything, so don't analyze it too much."

"Too late, I've already analyzed it."

"What have you figured out?"

"That I promised to teach you how to drive. I should've made it a rule."

"You and your rules."

We met eyes then, seeming to both remember the rules I'd made before: no attachments, no kissing. We were still good on both fronts. His gaze hadn't left mine. Weren't we?

"How is Jeff?"

I blinked, looking away from his intense stare. "What?"

"That's where you were, right? At the hospital."

I nodded. "Jeff's mom texted me last second and I had to go. He was asking for me."

Dax's shoulders went tense, but he said, "That's good."

I tried to figure out why Dax might not like that news. Why was he saying the opposite of what he was feeling? "He's still in pain, I guess. And will probably have to do physical therapy. So it will be a while before he goes home."

"Are you spelling out how much longer you need me around?"

"I . . . no. We're friends, right? You can . . . ."

He gave a breathy laugh, stopping me short. "It was a joke."

"Oh right." I leaned back against the bench. "But anyway, I was going to stay away from the hospital tomorrow, because it's Dallin's day."

"Dallin . . . the guy who blamed Jeff's accident on you."

"Right. I wanted to give him his time, but Jeff asked me to come. Made me promise. So I feel like I have to."

He leaned forward, put his elbows on his knees, and seemed to think. After a minute he said, "So you're trying to deal with anxiety by acting like you don't have it."

"What?"

"You know the hospital will stress you out tomorrow, especially with Dallin there."

"Yes."

"But instead of staying home for your own mental health, you're going to go there because someone else is expecting it."

"I can't stop living life."

"It's not something *you* want to do. You're worrying about someone else's emotions instead of your own."

"Either I'd be sitting at home worrying about Jeff wondering why I wasn't there or I'd be at the hospital worrying about Dallin being mad at me for being there."

"Because you haven't told them. If you told them you

had an anxiety disorder, they wouldn't wonder when you didn't show up for things or had to leave things early. And you wouldn't worry about them. They'd understand. They'd feel better and you'd feel better." He held up his hands and shook his head, like he was mad at himself for something. "You know what? Never mind. It's none of my business."

I let out a frustrated breath. "No. You're right. I'll tell them."

"Now you're just saying that because you think I'm mad."

"Are you?"

"It doesn't matter, Autumn." He put his hands on my cheeks. His hands were freezing. "Figure out what *you* think." His eyes went back and forth between mine. My temperature seemed to rise a couple degrees. "Figure out what you want," he said again, softer.

And then he was standing and walking away, and I just sat there and let him, not even offering him a ride. Maybe we both needed some space anyway. So we could follow the rules.

I pulled my knees up onto the bench with me, his words swirling in my mind. What he'd said made sense. I thought back to all the times even in the last couple of months when I went places to please others despite what I knew it would do to me—basketball games and parties and maybe even hospitals. It's not like I wanted to stop doing those things altogether, but I needed to read my own emotions better, not leave things *after* I freaked out but before. Stay healthy. But I didn't need to tell my friends about my anxiety in order to do that. I just needed to be better about standing up for myself. About not doing things I didn't want to do.

I slid my legs down to the floor and went to stand up when I saw Dax's book still sitting on the bench. He was long gone. I'd just give it to him at school the next day. I opened it up, curious, and sure enough the letter was still there. I read over the address again. Salt Lake. His mom lived that close and he hadn't seen her in years?

I pulled up the map app on my phone and entered her address into it. Fifty minutes away. I clicked the screen off and studied the envelope again. The return address was an unfamiliar one. Of course not his current address, but not the previous one either. I wondered how many times he'd had to move. How many families he'd had to live with.

The porch light was on and glowing a warm yellow as I headed up my front walkway. It looked so inviting. My home. I opened the door to the sounds of my family in the kitchen, laughing, dishes clinking. I shut the door behind me and went to join them. I stopped short, watching as my mom and brother stood around the island, picking at the leftover lasagna on the counter while my dad did the dishes.

"Let's make cookies," my brother said.

"You'll just eat all the cookie dough," my mom responded.

"And?"

"I want to eat all the cookie dough too," I said.

They all looked up. My brother spoke first. "It's about time you're home. Get in here and spend some quality time with me."

"So demanding." I set Dax's book on the counter and went to join them at the island. I pulled a fork out of the utensil drawer and dug into the leftover lasagna.

"How about a plate?" my mom said.

"There's salad too. It's in the fridge." Before I'd finished my bite of food, my dad was holding a gallon Ziploc of salad and my mom had a plate in her hand.

"Thanks." I took both and spent the next thirty minutes fielding questions about Jeff while we made cookies.

CHAPTER 36

● ● ● ● ● ● ●

If I hadn't promised Jeff, I wouldn't have been sitting in my car in the parking lot of the hospital trying to outlast Dallin. He'd been in there for at least an hour already. I could see his car parked two rows away from mine. I didn't want to take over his time. So I waited. This would keep me from a potentially anxiety-inducing confrontation. It was a good compromise, I thought.

It took him another forty-three minutes before he finally walked through the sliding glass doors and into the parking lot. I waited until he got into his car and drove away, then I went inside.

Mrs. Matson was in Jeff's room and Jeff was talking to her. I smiled. It was good to see him a little more coherent.

"Hello!" Mrs. Matson said when she saw me.

Jeff smiled. "Hey."

"Hi. You're awake."

"I'm on the front hours of my drugs instead of the last hours like yesterday. It helps."

I laughed.

He shifted in his bed, turning more toward me, and cringed. Drugs or not, he was obviously still in pain.

Mrs. Matson stood. "Here, have my seat. Dallin went to rescue my husband from up the street. He ran out of gas."

"Oh. He's coming back."

"It will be a party," Jeff said.

"Don't get too worked up," Mrs. Matson said. "I don't want the nurse yelling at you."

"I won't, Mom."

She left us alone and I sank slowly into the chair by his bed. I looked at Jeff, trying to read his expression. Had Dallin said anything about me? About what he'd accused me of the other day? Jeff seemed relaxed, happy, like he always did. He rarely had a different expression. I couldn't read Jeff very well. Hopefully, like me, Dallin didn't want to do anything that might upset him right now, while his body was still recovering.

"Hi," I said again.

He leaned back against the pillows.

"Any news on when you'll get out of here?"

"I guess when my oxygen level is better and I've proven I can walk."

"Can you?"

"I don't know. I start physical therapy tomorrow."

"Lucky you."

He twisted the tube hanging down by his arm once around his finger. "I can't wait to get out of here. We need to have an epic adventure as soon as possible. I was thinking tubing, but instead of sliding down the snow in tubes we go to the car graveyard and find old car parts to use, like a hood or a backseat. Tell me that wouldn't be fun."

That didn't sound like fun at all to me. My heart jumped just thinking about it. "Only if there's still snow when you're all better. Maybe we'll have to do that next year."

"It's happening this year."

The door creaked open.

Jeff lowered his voice and quickly whispered, "Play along with me for a sec."

I was confused.

Dallin walked in. "Dude, your dad does not know how to fill a jug of gas. He—" Dallin stopped immediately when he saw me there.

"He what?" Jeff asked.

"Nothing. He just couldn't."

"I'm glad you saved him. Should we think of a super-hero name for you?"

"I already have one."

Jeff's face went from smiling to worried as he stared toward the foot of his bed.

"What is it?" I asked.

"I . . . I can't feel my toes. Or my feet for that matter."

"What?" I stood, wondering if I should get the nurse when Jeff winked at me. Oh, was this what he meant earlier? I was supposed to play along with *this*?

He poked at his thigh. "I can't feel this either."

Dallin walked closer, concern in his eyes. I didn't think this was going to help our relationship right now.

He touched Jeff's foot. "Can you feel that?"

"Jeff," I said. "Not a good idea."

"No, I can't." Jeff picked up a pen from the table by his bed. "Autumn, stab my leg with this. Not hard, but enough to break the surface."

I rolled my eyes. He just went one step too far with this prank. Dallin would never believe that.

"Funny," I said, ready to clue Dallin in. "I'm not going to stab your leg with a pen."

Dallin stepped forward and swiped the pen out of

Jeff's hand. "I'll do it." And before I could blink, he swung his arm, pen and all, down onto Jeff's leg.

I screamed, throwing my hands over my mouth in shock. My eyes shot up to Jeff's face expecting to see pain, but there was only a big smile. Then he laughed. Then he coughed.

"We totally got you," he said. Dallin laughed as well.

"You guys are punks," I said, my heart still racing. I leaned against the table, trying to catch my breath.

"Why are you freaking out? It was a joke," Dallin said.

"I'm not. I . . ."

Jeff cringed through more coughing, his hand going to his side. He was clearly not well enough to do stupid stuff like that.

"Jeff, don't get too worked up," I said.

"I know, I know."

I sighed. I needed to leave. "I better get going."

"Autumn, it was all in good fun," Jeff said.

"I know. I'm not mad." Well, I sort of was. "But you need your rest." And I did too.

"You'll come back, right?"

"Yes. It's obvious you're getting bored in here."

"Mind-numbingly."

"Have a fun visit, Dallin," I said, but he just took over my seat without responding. Guess the prank hadn't improved anything between us. He was being such a baby, and I wanted to call him out on it, but not in front of Jeff. I had hoped that once Jeff started improving, Dallin would too, but that had obviously been too much to hope for.

CHAPTER 37

· · · · · · · ·

The tile floor was very white in the hospital and I wondered how they kept it clean with all the traffic. After leaving Jeff's room, I walked down two hallways, counting a hundred of those tiles until my nerves settled. I was thinking about different cleaning products they might have to use when a pair of feet stepped into my line of vision. I looked up and gasped.

"Dax? What are you doing here?" I glanced over my shoulder to see if we had an audience. When I saw we didn't, I hugged him, which did more to relax me than counting all hundred floor tiles had.

"Thought you might need your distraction," he said, hugging me back.

I laughed but then realized even with the smirk on his face that he was serious. "Wait, you're not visiting someone? You're really here for me?"

"You talked about promises and best friends fighting and you visiting on your off day—I don't know. I was hardly listening, but I sensed stress in your future."

He really came here for me. I was beyond shocked. "Hardly listening? Really? It sounds like you were listening perfectly."

"Don't get used to it." He stared down at me.

I hugged him again but quickly pulled away when I heard footsteps. Dallin walked by us, meeting my eyes and raising his eyebrows. He muttered *nice* under his breath and kept walking.

"Dallin," I called after him, "do you know Dax? He goes to our school. He volunteers at the hospital."

He half turned, gave a salute, and kept walking.

"Is this the boyfriend's best friend that hates your guts?"

"Yep."

He was silent for three beats, then said, "Did this help?"

I laughed without humor.

Still staring after Dallin, Dax said, "Volunteers at the hospital? You probably should've gone with mandatory community service. It might've been more believable."

"Not true."

"Do you want me to go threaten him to stay quiet about my philanthropic side?"

"No."

"Can we get out of here, then?"

I hesitated, wondered if I should go and tell Jeff about this before Dallin did. Downplay it. Or maybe a bigger downplay would be not to mention it at all and act like it was no big deal if Jeff brought it up.

Dax nodded once, his smile falling. "I'll leave."

"No," I said, determined. "Let's go."

We walked toward the exit. "How do you think they keep these floors clean?" I asked.

"A really good janitor?"

I smiled that he actually answered my question instead of making fun of me for it. "Did you take the bus all the way here?"

He nodded.

"How do you make money for bus fare?"

"The old-fashioned way."

"Holding up train conductors? Robbing banks?"

His smile was back, which was my goal. His hard-to-earn smiles made me feel like I did something not many others could.

"Mowing lawns. Washing windows."

"I was close." I clasped my hands together and offered him a bright smile. "The time has come."

"For what?"

"For you to learn how to drive."

My body jerked forward, my head almost hitting the dashboard. "Easy on the brakes. No need to stomp on them." We were in the school parking lot. It was the only place I could think of that was big enough and wouldn't have a lot of obstacles.

Dax eased off the brakes and the car rolled forward. He pushed on them again, and once again my body jerked forward. This time the seatbelt tightened and I let out a grunt.

"Sorry," he said. "Sorry." I'd never seen him more out of his element or unsure of himself. Dax was always a presence. A confident presence.

"It's okay. It takes a little while to get used to how sensitive the brake pedal can be."

"I suck at this. I'm going to ruin your car."

"You're not going to ruin my car." I wasn't sure if he understood what I said, though, since I was laughing so hard.

He shot me a look. "Is this going to be one of your laughing fits?"

I pointed back at the wheel. "Just drive. You'll get used to it."

"Driving or you laughing at me?"

"Both."

He inched forward again, his face a mixture of con-
centration and nerves. A surge of warm affection eased
through me. I felt like I knew Dax pretty well, but I still
wanted to know more about him.

"Where were you born?"

"Kaysville."

"How old were you when your dad left?"

"Four. Too young to really remember him much."

"And is that when your mom started . . ." I didn't want
to finish the sentence.

He did for me. "Doing drugs?"

"Yes."

"No. That was later, when her mother died."

"And when did CPS get involved?"

He rubbed his thumb over his left wrist. "When I was
thirteen."

"You're seventeen now?"

"Yes."

"Was she a good mom before all this?"

"She was the best mom she knew how to be."

"I guess that's all any of us can do." I reached over and
squeezed his knee.

"Are you trying to mess me up? Like in the Frisbee
throw?"

I smiled, remembering our library competition. "Is it
working?"

"We've already established you're a distraction."

I laid my hand back in my lap. My cheeks hurt from smiling. Dax circled the lot twice, getting steadier with each lap.

"How's the group home?" I asked.

"Have you ever felt trapped?"

I gave a single laugh. "Yes. I have anxiety."

"Right."

"I'm sorry you feel that way."

"Stop apologizing."

I stopped. "When I feel trapped, anxious, I think about the times I'm the happiest."

He dared take his eyes off the dark lot in front of him to level his gaze on me. The intensity in them took my breath away. Then he was focused again out the window. I almost apologized, thinking I had hit a nerve with that suggestion. But I held my tongue.

Dax's knuckles went white on the steering wheel and I looked out the windshield. Another car pulled into the parking lot at least fifty yards away. He slammed on the brakes, throwing me forward.

"Seriously, Dax. You're going to kill me."

"Isn't that what I've been trying to say?"

I laughed as I watched the car in front of us do a U-turn and exit the lot again. I laughed a lot around him, I realized. He made me happy. My insides felt like they were glowing, like I wanted to live in this moment forever. I played with the hot pink bracelet still firmly attached to my wrist and I took a deep breath and spit out, "You've definitely been added to the archive the last couple of weeks."

"What archive?" he asked.

"The happy memories one. The one I'll draw from in my dark times," I said quietly.

A smile stole away his hard expression before he wiped it off and pretended I hadn't seen it. But I had. And it got added to the bank.

"Happy memories can't get you through everything." He seemed to be talking from experience. He stopped the car and put it in Park, then turned toward me. "Did I leave my book at the park yesterday?"

"Yes. I have it. I forgot. I'll bring it to school on Monday."

"Okay."

I leaned my head on the seat, staring at him. His eyes held mine. They were intense. I'd never felt so exposed before. Like he was looking into me.

"What?" he asked.

"Thanks for coming tonight. I needed it."

"Sure." He ran a single finger along the line of my jaw and I shivered.

"You're always cold," he said.

My eyes stared into his. "I'm not cold."

He was close. Too close. But I didn't back away. In

fact, maybe I had been the one to close the distance between us. I stopped myself from leaning in any closer. I breathed in his breath. Then it was him moving forward, his lips seconds from meeting mine.

"We made a rule," I whispered.

"Unlike you, I don't follow rules." He didn't give me a chance to respond. His lips met mine and stole my willpower. I pressed closer to him. I tried to move my right hand to his hair but the seatbelt prevented me from getting closer. I searched blindly for the release button, not willing to separate myself from him to find it. He was faster. He unlatched my belt, then pulled me closer.

My hands found his hair, his neck, his shoulders. His hands found my hips, lifting and sliding me across the center console and onto his lap. There wasn't enough room between him and the steering wheel but that didn't stop me. My elbows rested on his shoulders as our kiss deepened.

And then a horn sounded, loud and long. I gasped and pulled away. It was me, I realized. My back was pushing on the horn. I laughed, maneuvering myself back into my own seat. Silence filled the air. My lips felt swollen, my cheeks hot.

"You're in for it now," I said, buckling my seatbelt again. "Attachment is in your future. I warned you."

He smiled and opened the car door. When he arrived

at the passenger door and opened it for me, I realized we needed to switch places. I needed to drive. How was I going to drive? How was I even going to walk around the car with my wobbly legs? When I stepped out, he didn't move for me to walk around, though. He pressed me against the car and kissed me again, his warm hands over my ears. I went up on my tiptoes in answer. His warmth poured through my body and I felt like I would explode from happiness. I finally pushed on his chest, breaking the kiss. I was feeling too much, too fast.

Somehow I drove him home, wobbly legs and all, us barely speaking two words. When I pulled to a stop in front of the group home, he leaned over and brushed a kiss on my cheek, then another across my lips.

"See you," he said in a gravelly voice, and was gone.

CHAPTER 38

• • • • • • •

had kissed Dax. What did that mean? Did he want to be together? Did I? My head spun all night long with these thoughts and others. So many that my brain felt like it was going to explode. Guilt twisted my stomach until it felt like I was going to be sick. I tried to tell myself that Jeff and I weren't together, were never together so there was no need to feel guilty. But I liked Jeff. I had been planning on being with Jeff for months, nearly a year now. Whatever was going on between me and Dax couldn't happen. Not to mention if I walked away from Jeff now, everyone would hate me. All my friends would think I was a jerk. Dallin would only be proven right. Did Dax even want me to walk away from Jeff? Did kissing mean anything to him or was it just another distraction? I was so glad it was the weekend because I hardly slept at all.

The next morning I pulled down a bowl from the cupboard, feeling like a zombie. My mom had a pot of oatmeal ready on the stove and I dished myself two spoonfuls. She came humming into the kitchen as I added my fifth scoop of brown sugar.

"Did you want some oatmeal with your sugar?" she asked.

"Funny, Mom," I said, taking one more scoop, then stirring it in until my oatmeal turned brown.

"You look tired," she said.

My chest was tight with the familiar feeling of anxiety. "I am."

"Everything okay?"

No, I wanted to scream. But then what? "I just have an unsolvable problem."

"Something I can help you with?"

"I wish."

"Try me. Your mom is good at finding solutions."

I looked around in jest. "My mom? Then I better go find her."

"There's nothing wrong with speaking in the third person."

"I'm fine, Mom. Really." This was something only time could solve.

Owen brushed by me in the hall on my way to the bathroom. "It's been so nice seeing you this week, sis."

I knew he was being sarcastic. I had hardly been home at all and it was already Saturday and he was irritated. "Sorry." I felt like I was always apologizing to someone. "Let's hang out now."

"Can't. I actually made plans."

My phone rang, Lisa's name flashing across the screen. "Hello," I answered.

"Hi! Today is my hospital day and I want you to come with me."

I closed my eyes. Now was the time to say no, when I knew I should stay home. But then I thought about the hour and a half we'd have in the car there and back and how I really needed to talk to someone, so I found myself saying, "Okay."

A light snow hit the windshield as Lisa and I drove on the freeway to the hospital. The heater in Lisa's car had stopped working, so the defroster was blasting cold air, and we were both shivering. I wrapped my scarf around my neck three times, then said, "I kissed Dax." It probably wasn't the greatest of conditions to tell someone something surprising. The car only swerved a little with her reaction, however, and she corrected it quickly.

"What? When?"

"Last night. We kissed."

"So . . . not a distraction anymore?"

"I don't know."

"Because of Jeff?"

"I don't know. I don't know how I feel about anyone right now."

"I thought you were in love with Jeff before the accident."

"Not in love . . . definitely in like."

"I think Dax screwed you up. If he wasn't in the picture, you'd know exactly how you felt."

She was probably right about that. "You think?"

"You've known Dax for weeks, Autumn. Weeks. You've known Jeff for years. Dax is just some new shiny toy. Jeff is someone who fits with you. Who fits with all of us."

"I feel like I need to tell Jeff about last night, though. About what happened with Dax. I don't want to be dishonest."

"I think you should think about it longer. Decide what you really want. Before you talk to Jeff."

"Do you hate me?" I asked.

"No! Why would I hate you?"

"I don't know. Jeff is so likable and everyone loves him and I did something stupid."

"Autumn." She reached over and squeezed my hand. "You're my best friend. I would never hate you. I'm team Autumn all the way. No matter what you decide I'll be on your side."

Jeff's mom, like she often did, greeted us with a hug when we arrived. "He has a surprise for you," she said.

"A surprise?"

"Come on." She led us to his hospital room door. "Wait here."

We stood in the hall as she disappeared into his room.

"What do you think the surprise is?" Lisa asked.

"No idea."

A few minutes later, the door opened and Jeff was sitting in a wheelchair. "Look who can get around now."

He looked so much more alert and awake. The drugs they had pumped into his system after the accident must've been mostly worked out. "That's awesome," I said.

"Go stand at the end of the hall."

"What?"

"Walk to the end of the hall and wait there." He shooed us away with a wave of his hand.

Lisa and I both followed his directions, walking until we were about forty feet away, then turning to face him. His mom moved behind his wheelchair and pointed it in our direction. He bent down and lifted the footrests, then stood.

"You're not going to tell him about Dax now, are you?" Lisa asked under her breath.

"Not on your life."

Lisa gave me a sympathetic smile and then turned back to Jeff. "That's so amazing."

"Wait for it," he called. Then he walked several unsure steps in our direction. Steps that made me want to rush forward and take his arm so he didn't fall. But I noticed his mom hovering off to the left of him, there to assist if he needed it, so I held my ground. He made it all the way to us, then wrapped me up in a hug, leaning a little against me for support.

I patted his back. "I'm so proud of you." And I was. So proud. I needed to be there for him as he finished out his recovery. Me telling him I was unsure of where we stood or how I felt wouldn't be helpful right now. That could wait. Or maybe I'd figure out my feelings and realize Jeff and I were meant to be.

In the time it took for the hug, his mom had already positioned the wheelchair behind him and I helped him sit down. He was beaming.

"Can the girls take me for a walk around the hospital, Mom?" he asked.

"Of course. Be good," she said, pointing her finger at him like she knew the kind of trouble Jeff could get into.

He just smiled up at her in innocence. "I'm always good, Mom."

CHAPTER 39

. . . .

"Okay, Autumn, sit on my lap, and Lisa, push the wheel-chair as hard as you can," Jeff said.

We were outside of the hospital now. It had stopped snowing and we'd pushed Jeff and his chair up the side-walk to a park the hospital built. He had decided the sidewalk was just wide enough and had just the right amount of decline that it would create the perfect speed ramp.

I pointed at the swings in the play equipment. "Wouldn't you rather try that out? It's especially built for wheelchairs."

"Are you chicken, Autumn?"

"Yes, actually. That pole down there looks like it would be very painful to crash my head into."

He positioned his wheelchair. "I'm going with or without you so you might as well protect me."

"With my body?"

"I won't let you get hurt."

There were so many things wrong with this scenario, the least of which was climbing onto a recovering patient's lap. Lisa held her tongue during the whole exchange and when I looked at her for help she seemed to sense my discomfort and said, "I'll try first so we can see if it's safe."

"Nope, me and Autumn first."

Lisa widened her eyes at me, almost like telling me to say no.

I opened my mouth to do just that but then made the mistake of looking at Jeff's hopeful face and said, "Fine."

Jeff patted his lap with both his hands.

I put one hand on the armrest. "I feel like I'm going to hurt you. Are your legs in pain?"

"No. My legs are uninjured. You will not hurt me."

I took a deep breath and climbed on his lap.

"Ouch." He sucked a breath between his teeth.

I jumped off but he caught my wrist with a laugh. "I'm just kidding," he said. "Sit down."

My heart was in my throat, and it had been so long

since I'd been a part of one of Jeff's "adventures" that I'd forgotten this was how I always felt during them—on the verge of panic.

I sat anyway, putting one arm around his shoulder and my other awkwardly propped behind me, holding on to the armrest. Beads of sweat were forming along my upper lip as I imagined careening off the sidewalk and re-injuring Jeff all over again. His mom was going to kill me.

He reached down to the right, undoing the wheel lock. "Okay, Lisa, give us a shove."

She reached for the handles and gave me one last look as if asking me if I really wanted to do this. I closed my eyes and nodded. I felt the wheelchair lurch forward. Then I opened my eyes so I could see if at any point I would need to jump off. "You're dead to me," I mumbled to Jeff.

He just wrapped an arm around my waist and laughed.

When we started to pick up speed Jeff's laugh tapered off into a nervous chuckle. That didn't help my already active imagining of how this would end. As if on cue, we reached the flat section of the sidewalk and hit a bump that made the wheelchair catch a half second of air. We landed, our heads smashing together. The chair finally stopped when it hit a patch of grass at the very edge of the sidewalk.

"Are you okay?" I asked, jumping off his lap and examining his head where mine had collided against it.

"I'm fine. I have a hard head."

My temple throbbed but I resisted the urge to reach up and rub it. I hoped it didn't bruise or swell. I must have succeeded in playing it off because he didn't ask if I was hurt.

Lisa came running down after us. "Are you okay?" she asked. I thought she was looking at Jeff, but she was asking me.

"I'm fine. It's fine."

Jeff put his hands in the air. "Push me back up. It's your turn, Lisa."

"I don't think it's a good idea," I said. Surely a guy who just had a head injury shouldn't take this risk.

"You're ruining the fun," he said.

I tried to think if anyone had ever said no to Jeff's exploits before his accident. He was always suggesting crazy adventures and we always went along, my anxiety in tow.

"I'll push you on the swing," I suggested again.

"After one more trip with Lisa."

And it went exactly like he wanted. First the trip down the hill, me standing at the top, my worry keeping them safe, then him and his wheelchair on the specially designed swing.

I could tell he was tired but it took another ten minutes for me to convince him we should head back.

"This is the most fun I've had in a while," he said as we wheeled him back toward his room. "I don't want it to end."

"It's not your last day of fun, Jeff," I said. "There will be many more. You need to take it easy."

"Yes, Mommy," he said, but reached back and patted my hand.

I *had* felt like his mom for the last hour and I didn't like it. I didn't like being the one who had to speak reason, but someone needed to.

We made it back to his room, and delivered him back to his real mom and left.

CHAPTER 40

. . . .

My mom was waiting in my room when I arrived home.
"Hey, what's up?" I asked.

She tilted her head, inspecting the side of my fore-head. "What happened?"

"What?" I reached up and felt a swollen bump from where Jeff and I had collided. "Oh. Wheelchair games gone wrong. Where are Dad and Owen?"

"Indoor golf."

"Is Owen mad at me? I haven't had much time with him this week."

"He'll be fine. How are *you*, Autumn?"

"I'm okay." Then decided to be honest because I knew she could tell. "A bit overstressed lately."

"I thought so. Maybe it's time to take a break. Take a couple of days off the hospital and friends and school. Just decompress at home."

It did sound good, but it wouldn't get me out of my head.

"You've been taking your medication, right?"

"Yes." I couldn't imagine how much worse I might feel without it right now. "I think most of this stuff is situational, and I'm hoping that when Jeff is out of the hospital things will feel right again."

"You're questioning your feelings for him?"

"I'm questioning everything."

"There's nothing wrong with thinking things through. But it's important to make the decision that's right for you."

"He's in the hospital."

She smiled. "I know. And that makes you feel guilty. But regardless, you have to live your life, not his."

"I know. Thanks, Mom."

I unlaced my shoes and was stepping out of them as she headed for the door. "Oh," I called after her. "Have you seen a book? *Hamlet*? I left it in the kitchen the day before yesterday."

"I think it's still there."

"Thanks." I kicked my shoes into my closet and went to the kitchen in my socked feet. The book sat on the counter and I picked it up. Almost out of habit now, I flipped through the pages, looking for the letter. It wasn't there. I flipped through them again, not producing a different result.

"Mom!" This wasn't good. I searched the countertops. There was a pile of mail next to the phone and I looked through it but couldn't find anything. I scanned the floor under the cabinets, even pulled out the trash can and started digging through it.

My mom came into the kitchen. "What are you doing?"

"There was a letter. I'm missing a letter."

"Calm down. We'll find it. What did it look like?"

"Like a letter. A long white envelope with writing on it." My hand met the slimy remains of macaroni and cheese. I shook it off and turned on the sink, washing my hands with soap. I needed an empty bag so that I could transfer the trash over. I headed for the pantry.

"Did it have a stamp on it?"

I stopped and slowly turned to look at my mom's worried face.

"Yes . . . why?"

"I thought you were looking for a letter. Like a piece of paper with writing on it."

"No . . . so did you see it?"

"I sent it."

"You *what*?"

"It was just sitting there on the counter addressed and ready to go. I thought maybe one of Owen's friends or one of your friends needed it mailed."

"No, it was in the book."

She lowered her brows. "No, it wasn't in a book. Just on the counter."

It must've slipped out. "Oh no. He's going to kill me."

"Who's going to kill you?"

"When did you mail it? Yesterday?"

"Yes."

"It was only going to Salt Lake. Do you think it got there yet?"

"Probably."

"Crap. Crap, crap, crap." A saving thought came to me. "I have her address. In my phone. I entered it into my phone." I rushed back to my room and pulled my shoes back on. "I have to go talk to her."

"Go talk to who?" my mom asked from my doorway.

"His mom. I have to go talk to her. Maybe she'll give me the letter back. I'm going to fix this."

"Autumn, I don't think you should go anywhere with how you're feeling right now."

"Mom, please. If I don't I'm going to freak out. Like

really freak out. Can you just trust me on this? I need to do something."

"Show me your hands."

I held them out in front of me. Surprisingly they were as steady as could be.

She nodded. "Call me on your way home."

"Okay. Thank you!" I kissed her cheek and ran out the door.

CHAPTER 41

●　　●　　●　　●　　●　　●

The apartment complex was in a scary part of Salt Lake. It was a good thing my mom hadn't known exactly where I was going because there was no way she'd have let me go there. The other good thing was that it was still early afternoon so it wasn't as scary as it might've been when the sun went down.

I walked through the glass front doors and up a wide set of stairs. The elevator looked functional at best so I continued to take the stairs up to the fourth floor. The hall smelled like mildew and cinnamon, making me gag a little. I stepped over a tipped-over planter box halfway down the hall, dirt spilled across the carpeted floor. When I arrived in front of her door, I wiped my sweating palms on my jeans and knocked.

The woman who opened the door had graying hair and Dax's eyes. *Please let this go well*, I thought. "Hi."

"Can I help you?"

I looked over her shoulder and into the apartment. Maybe I'd see a stack of mail somewhere. I didn't. All I saw was a tidy studio apartment. A small couch with a knit quilt hanging over the back. A bookcase with neatly stacked books. A kitchen with wiped-down counters and a teakettle on the stove. Everything in its place. I didn't know what I had been expecting, but not this. Not a clear-eyed, healthy-looking woman with a tidy studio apartment. "Um. Did you get your mail today?"

She let out a small gasp and I knew she had. I knew she knew I was there because of it.

"My mom sent you that letter by accident. He's not ready for any sort of response right now. Can you respect that?"

She opened the door wider. "Come in."

I did. We sat on the couch together. Me desperate, her calm. Like Dax.

"You know my son," she said.

"I do. He left a book at my house with that letter in it. He has no idea you have it."

She smiled a sad smile. "Too good to be true."

"You were going to write him back?"

"Of course. I already started to." She picked up a paper off the coffee table next to us that I hadn't been able to see from the door. She pulled out Dax's envelope from beneath it. The edge was jagged from where she had opened it. She ran her finger over the return address. "I had no idea where he was."

"He's not there anymore. He lives in a different house."

She nodded. "How is he?"

"He's . . ." My heart thudded several hard beats. "Amazing. You have an amazing son."

She looked back up at me. "You're his girlfriend. I didn't realize."

"No. I'm not. Dax doesn't . . ." *He doesn't do commitment* is what I almost said, but instead finished with, "Doesn't want that."

"I'm sorry."

She obviously knew I did want something with Dax. And I did, I realized, as I was sitting there desperate to get the letter back for him. Desperate to fix this. I finally knew what I wanted, and it felt bittersweet in that moment.

"So what do you need from me . . . ?"

She was waiting for my name. "Autumn," I provided.

"Autumn. What can I do?"

"Not send whatever it is you're writing. Not yet, at

298

least. Will you give me a week to tell him what happened?"

"Of course." She smiled, and I saw Dax inherited that from her as well. "But then I can send this to him, right? I have changed so much, and I'd like him to see that. Plus, he has legitimate questions in here. Questions he needs the answers to even if he wants nothing to do with me."

"Yes. You should send it in a week."

She picked up the pen lying on the coffee table. "Will you write down where I should send it to?" She handed the pen to me.

I stared at the pen. Maybe I should just let her send it to the address listed on his envelope. It would possibly get forwarded on to him eventually. But that was just putting off the inevitable. Either way I was going to have to tell him what I'd done when I returned his book without a letter. This way, with a letter from her in hand, he'd see that his mom had changed. This woman wasn't the same one who'd walked away from Dax. And with that tattoo branded on his arm, he never would've sent the letter on his own. Things happen for a reason. Maybe this did. Maybe it would help him with his commitment issues. With me.

I took the pen and envelope. "Why haven't you reached out to him in all these years?"

"I didn't deserve to. I was waiting for him. Autumn, I

still remember the day the police showed up at my house to take him from me. One officer had my meth, the other had my son. Do you know which officer I lunged for? I did not deserve to be the first to reach out. But now I know that he wanted to. That he's been thinking about me as well."

My throat went tight with that story, reminded me what she had done, who my loyalty was to. I handed her back her things. "I don't have his address memorized."

She seemed to know I wasn't being honest. She held up the letter. "He asked about his dad, too. He needs to know."

I nodded. "I'll send it to you after I talk to him." Or better yet, I'd let him reach out. I had a week to tell him what I'd done, and hopefully he'd take it well and want his mom's letter. "Do you have a number we can reach you at?"

She nodded and wrote it down on a piece of scratch paper.

I tucked it into my pocket and smiled. "It was nice to meet you."

"You too, Autumn."

"And then she said, Owen, you are the handsomest, smartest, funniest guy in the entire universe."

I looked up from where I had been staring at the menu at Owen's favorite café. Okay, maybe I'd been staring *past* the menu. "She really said that?"

He threw the wrapper from his straw at me. "I've waited all week and you're still not really hanging out with me."

"I'm sorry. I'm sorry. But do you see that?" I pointed to the space above my head.

"No."

"Well, I feel it. It's a ticking time bomb. It's ticking down to the moment I hand Dax his book back with no letter in it."

"And when will that be?"

"Never? Can I just not ever tell him?"

"The sooner you tell him, the less anxious you'll feel about it."

I'd filled my brother in on what had happened. Mainly because my mom told him and my dad the story about the letter and they all wanted context when I got home. Now it was a full day later, and I couldn't shake the dread of talking to Dax about what I'd done. "I know."

"Should I take you by his house?"

"No." I patted my menu. "No, you're leaving tonight. I have time to talk to him. So finish your story. This girl you were telling me about, she's obviously very wise if she said all those things about my brother. I approve."

"She didn't exactly say them, but I saw them in her eyes."

I laughed. "I bet you did."

"And I know she's the one for me," he said in a dramatic fashion.

I wanted to laugh again, but I stopped. "You know? Just like that?"

"Well, not just like that, but it was almost that easy. Shouldn't love be easy?"

"You love her?"

"No, but I just mean the act of falling in love. Shouldn't it be easy?"

"Yes. It definitely shouldn't be scripted."

"Exactly. It's not something you should have to analyze over and over again. If it's right, you should know."

I smiled and shut my menu, looking around for the waiter. "Now you're the love expert?"

"Always have been, Autumn."

It wasn't that I was doubting what I had come to realize at Dax's mom's house. I knew I liked Dax. I just wished that Owen had met him. I wanted one second opinion. Everyone else was on Jeff's side.

The thought of Dax holding my face at the park and saying *figure out what you think* flashed through my mind. His eyes staring into mine so intensely. I didn't need other people to tell me what I already knew.

"I know what I think," I said out loud.

Owen looked up from his menu. "Oh yeah?"

"I like him. A lot."

"Dax?"

"Yes," I said.

"And you don't care about the friend fallout that will occur with that choice?"

"I don't care."

He smiled. "Good for you."

"Regardless of what happens with Dax, Jeff isn't right for me. I wanted him to be for so long that I looked past the way he made me feel when I was with him—always on edge, worrying what he'd do or say next. I didn't notice the difference until I met someone who helps me relax." Now I just needed to make sure I hadn't ruined everything. And I needed to tell him how I felt. That wouldn't be an easy task either, to convince the boy who didn't do commitment that we could be different. I twisted the pink bracelet on my wrist. But I had to try.

CHAPTER 42

. . . .

On Monday as I grabbed *Hamlet* off my nightstand, I contemplated for the millionth time what today would be like. The full-length mirror on the back of my door showed me how nervous I felt about what I was about to do. I was about to hand Dax his book back without the letter inside. It was going to be how I started the conversation. Maybe I'd take him to the greenhouse again. Who cares if we had to miss first period? We would talk this out. Then I'd tell him I liked him.

I straightened my green sweater, one of my favorites, and fixed one of my loose waves. Yes, I had put extra care into my looks today. There was nothing wrong with trying to distract the guy while delivering shocking news.

But Dax wasn't by the buses where I normally saw him in the mornings. And a search of the school hallways produced the same results. I rounded the corner, thinking I'd try looking in his first period class, when I nearly ran over Dallin.

"Autumn," he said, all business.

"Yes, Dallin?"

"It's your day today at the hospital. You're still planning on going, right?"

"Actually today is kind of bad for me. Do you know if anyone might want to switch?"

"Seriously? You hanging out with someone else?" He gave me the same smug look he'd given me in the hospital when he saw me with Dax.

"No, it's just . . ." That's exactly what I was planning to do. "Never mind. I'll go." I needed to talk to Jeff anyway. I could talk to him first.

"No, if you're too good to be assigned a day, then I can find someone else."

"Dallin. Just stop, okay? I'll go."

He held up his hands in surrender. "Good. Because despite everything, Jeff seems to like you."

"You're kind of a jerk, you know that?"

"Only when I think someone is screwing over my friend."

I wanted to argue, but I *was* about to screw over his friend and that made my insides twist with guilt. I had to remind myself that it was my life I had to live. Nobody else's. I was going to talk to Jeff today.

Jeff and his parents were playing a board game when I walked into the room. I knew Jeff was humoring them by the look on his face. The tray that extended over his bed was too small for the board, but Life was spread out there as well as possible.

"Autumn!" he said, and the little car with its peg people fell onto his lap.

"Hi."

"Come play with us." He plopped a little green car onto the board and added a pink person to it. I pulled up a chair and his dad handed me a stack of money and a career card. *Teacher*, it said. Forty-seven thousand dollars of salary. The structure of the game calmed my nerves a bit, and before long I was laughing with Jeff.

"I want to change careers," he announced ten minutes later, when he landed on that square.

"But you're a surgeon and you have the highest salary possible in the game," I said.

"I do not base my decisions on salary, Autumn. I base them on job satisfaction and I'm unsatisfied. I'm away from my wife and twins too much. I need a change in my life."

His mom laughed. "You should always be happy in your job choice. What a wise decision."

"There's something to be said about security, too," I said.

"Very true," Jeff's dad agreed.

"Do you hear that, parents? Autumn is a gold digger. If I don't bring her home lots of money, she'll be unhappy."

"Sorry, Jeff, but I'm in my own car with my own blue-peg husband, and I bring home a teacher's salary. Abandoning your surgeon career is not going to affect me."

He flung the surgeon card at me like a Frisbee. "It's totally going to affect you."

"What do you really want to be when you grow up?" I asked, realizing this was something else I didn't know about him.

"A dirt bike racer."

"Really?"

"No, but that sounds fun. Maybe I'll do that on the side."

"What do *you* want to do when you grow up?" Mr. Matson asked me.

"I think I want to be a psychologist." Because that was safe and secure and not risky at all. But it was more than that too. My psychologist had helped me so much over the years that I wanted to help others.

"I didn't know that," Jeff said. "I thought you'd do something with photography."

"Yeah I . . ."

"Psychology is a good choice," his dad said. "Jeff needs to decide."

"Oh please, I'm seventeen. I have my whole life in front of me."

His mom patted his arm. "Yes, you do. We're lucky."

Sitting here in the hospital with his family, I couldn't help but think that he really was lucky that he had survived the car accident and was going to be fine. We were both going to be fine.

A man in a long white coat walked in the room. "It's time for your daily torture," he said. "Blood tests and physical therapy."

"But my girl is here. Can't it wait?"

His girl? Did he just call me his girl? Surely he hadn't decided that without talking to me first. Not that it would surprise me. Jeff seemed to do a lot of things without thinking about them first.

"I'll give you thirty minutes," he said.

"Thirty minutes. That means all adults out of the room," Jeff said.

His mom smiled but cleaned up the board and stacked it off to the side, next to the baseball bat from Dallin. And get well cards, and drawings I was just now noticing. I'd never brought him anything. My stomach began tensing up in anticipation of being alone with Jeff and the talk we needed to finally have.

The door clicked behind his exiting parents and I turned to face him.

"How is physical therapy going?"

"I've aged sixty years in two weeks. I need a walker and an oxygen tank."

"And your pain? How is that?"

"Once-a-day pain meds, doc. Why so serious?"

Because I didn't want to face what else I had to talk about. I wasn't even sure how to start. Maybe I didn't have to. Maybe he already had some of the information. "Have you talked to Dallin?"

"Yes, Friday. Surely you remember us being idiots."

"I remember. You haven't talked to him since then?"

"No, why?"

I took a gulp of air. "Do you know Dax? From school?"

He scrunched his face up as though thinking. "Dax Miller? The druggie?"

"He's not a druggie."

"What about him?"

"Well, he was in the library with—"

The door swung open and Dallin walked in with an "I heard you're springing this joint on Wednesday."

My gaze swung from Jeff to Dallin, then back again. "You get to go home on Wednesday? You didn't tell me."

"I was just about to. Hey, Autumn, I get to go home on Wednesday."

"That's great. Really great."

"I agree," Jeff said.

"I do too." Dallin slid a rolling chair across the room and sat down opposite me, next to Jeff. "So, Friday night is the basketball game, but Saturday night I am throwing you a Jeff is Free party. My place. You in?"

Jeff smiled. "Since my name is in the title, I better be."

"Isn't that too much for you too soon?" I asked.

"Have you met my doctor, Dallin? Doctor Autumn."

"Funny, but I'm serious."

He grabbed my hand. "I know you are. I'll be fine." Then he turned to Dallin. "Is there still snow on that hill in your backyard? We need to go by the car graveyard before Saturday."

"Yes, and yes."

So much for talking to him today. I had a feeling Dallin was here on purpose. I had interrupted his day so he was paying me back. It was fine, though—my talk with Jeff could wait. Maybe until after the celebratory party. Jeff was having an exciting week. I didn't need to ruin it.

CHAPTER 43

• • • • • • •

Dax was standing in my driveway when I pulled up. An embarrassing amount of relief poured through my body. He was there. I needed him and he was there. Then I remembered what I had to talk to him about first, before I got to tell him he was amazing. My eyes shot to his book that sat on the console of my car. I tucked it between the seats and rolled down my window.

"Hop in." I didn't want to risk my parents interrupting us.

He listened, climbing in the passenger seat, and I drove, with no destination in mind.

"I was worried you were sick today. I didn't see you at school. I'm so happy to see you. I've had the weirdest day. The weirdest couple of days, actually. I need to talk it out." I put my hand on his but he didn't grab on or move in any way. His gaze was directed out the window. His stare was dark.

"You didn't want me to go inside and meet your family?" he asked.

"What? No, I did. I do. I'd love for you to meet them, but I needed to talk to you."

"Pull over up here." He gestured toward a business complex ahead. I pulled into the parking lot, coming to a stop in front of a dentist office.

"Did something happen? Is everything okay at the group home? Are you okay?" I slid closer and put my arms around his shoulders, brushed a kiss on his cheek. If he needed to get his mind off something, I would gladly help. I could use some mind clearing myself. He was as still as could be, not moving to welcome me in at all, not even uncrossing his arms from in front of his chest.

"Dax? What is it?" I pulled at his arms playfully.

"You saw my mom."

"Oh." *Oh.* All this rage was directed at *me.* I sank back into my own seat. Who had told him? I was supposed to be the one to tell him. I had the gentlest way possible planned out. "Yes?"

"You sent her my letter?"

"No . . . I didn't. My mom did by accident. It had fallen out of the book. She saw it on the counter so she sent it. I'm so sorry."

"But you just happened to have memorized the address on the envelope?"

"No, I put it in my phone when I found it because I was curious about where she lived. And then when the letter was sent . . . It probably sounds unbelievable but I promise it was not some preplanned plot or anything. It was all just a big accident."

"But you preplan everything. Make rules for everything."

"No, not everything."

He wouldn't look at me, just stared out the front windshield like it was all he could do to control his anger. "You getting in your car and driving to my mother's house was an accident?"

"Well . . . not that part. By that time I was just trying to fix the mistake."

"*That* was the mistake."

"I know." My chest was tight, my breath hard to come by. I did not want to use that as an excuse not to have this conversation, though, so I tried to hold myself together.

"Who told you?"

"She did."

I gasped. "Your mom? She told you? She went to your house?"

"Yes. Letter in hand, telling me all about her new friend Autumn."

"How did she find you?"

"Followed the address forwarding trail."

"But she wasn't supposed to do that. She said she just wanted to send you a letter with important stuff that you'd need to know about yourself. And she was going to wait until I got back to her. She was going to wait until I could talk to you first."

"She lies. All the time. Whatever it takes to get what she wants."

"I'm so sorry. I just wanted to fix things."

"Why?" He finally looked at me and I wanted him to look away. There was so much hate there.

"I don't know. I wanted to help." A single tear spilled out and I wiped it away quickly. "She said she'd changed. I . . ." What was I thinking?

"I am not your secret little charity case, Autumn."

"Secret? You're not a secret."

"Aren't I, though?"

"I . . ." Not on purpose. I thought he hadn't wanted to be seen with me at school. "I told Lisa about you . . . about us. And my brother."

"Stay out of my business," he said. "You said just a

distraction. No attachments. This is way beyond attachment if you feel the need to try to fix my life."

I nodded, more tears spilling over. "Don't worry, you
just cured me of any attachment."

He opened the car door, got out, and slammed it
behind him. Then he walked away. I stayed there, my
heart hurting so bad it felt like someone was squeezing it
in their fist. I didn't leave until I calmed my racing heart
and cried away all my tears and any feelings I had about
Dax with them. Maybe he had done me a favor.

CHAPTER 44

• • • • • • •

The texting started the next morning as I lay in bed, taking a mental health day. Or maybe it was a broken heart day. Either way, I needed some time off, and my mom agreed.

Lisa: Where are you?

Me: Not feeling well, staying home for a couple of days.

Lisa: Oh no! Can I bring you soup?

Me: No, I'll be better soon.

Lisa: Hopefully by this weekend because it should be epic.

Wednesday.

Jeff: I got out of the hospital today! Can you come see me? I'm bored.

Me: Congrats! I can't come today. I stayed home from school. But maybe I'll come by your house tomorrow.

Thursday.

Lisa: Are you still sick? I'll wear a mask if you let me come visit.

Me: No mask needed. I'm feeling a lot better.

Lisa: Yay! Just in time for the basketball game tomorrow.

Me: Not sure if I'm going to that.

Lisa: Jeff will be there.

Me: Is Dallin still throwing him the party on Saturday?

Lisa: Yes.

Me: I'll try to come to that. I'll probably skip the basketball game.

Lisa: Why?

Me: Believe me, it's a good choice.

A couple of hours later as I lay wrapped in my down comforter watching a movie, I got another text.

Jeff: I thought you were coming over today.

Me: Stayed home again.

Jeff: You okay?

Me: Feeling a lot better.

Jeff: Good. I miss you.

I swallowed the lump in my throat. I missed him too. Just like I missed all my friends. But that was all it was.

Friendship. And I needed to tell him that. Maybe that was another reason I had stayed home all week. I was good at avoidance.

Friday.

"Are you sure you're going to be okay here alone?" my mom asked. She was all dressed up and heading off to her work party with my dad.

"I'm positive." I tugged on my fingers. "I'm sorry I'm not going with you. I promised Dad I would when he told me I could go up to the cabin."

She smiled. "Oh please, this would be like torture for you. Besides, you didn't end up at the cabin, so you're breaking no promises."

"This is true."

"How are you feeling?"

"Better. Thanks for letting me stay home this week."

"Of course. You need to take care of yourself."

"I know. That's why I'm staying home from the basketball game tonight too. Just the thought of it makes me cringe."

"There's nothing wrong with that. I think you sometimes worry too much what your friends will think if you don't go somewhere and not enough about how you're feeling."

"I know. Well, now I know. I'm working on it."

Dax had been wrong. I hadn't needed to make a big announcement about my anxiety to my friends, I just needed to learn how to say no to them and take better care of myself.

She patted my cheek. "I love you, kid. Be good."

"I will."

The doorbell rang at 6:45 and I thought about not answering it. I wasn't expecting anyone and I didn't want to talk to a salesperson. But then it rang again, and I sighed and walked to the front door. When I opened it, I saw one second of Dallin's smiling face before he threw a pillowcase over my head.

I screamed and tried to pull it off but then my hands were bound to my sides by some sort of rope or tape.

"Your presence has been requested," Dallin said. "You are being kidnapped."

"Dallin, please don't do this. This is not cool." I could already feel my pulse picking up speed, my chest tightening. It's just Dallin, I told myself. I'll be fine. But that logic didn't help. It was the pillowcase over my head. I needed it off. I felt smothered, trapped, confined. "Take it off. Please. I'm not one of your stupid guy friends." I knew he'd done this to Zach before. At the movies. He was just doing what he did. But I couldn't handle it like Zach.

Dallin directed me on my shuffling feet to a vehicle that I could hear was already on. A door opened and he delivered me inside. I wasn't sure if the other guys were inside—Zach or Connor.

"Can someone please just take the pillowcase off? I'm going to get sick." My stomach hurt and I was worried I really was going to get sick.

There was the tiniest laugh but nobody helped me. The radio turned on and the car started moving. Nobody had put on my seatbelt.

"I need a seatbelt," I said.

"A seatbelt?" The voice was right next to my ear, then another voice behind me said the same thing. They were loud, distorted. But someone buckled me in.

Throughout the ride the different voices yelled out stupid things. Things like, "Don't run the stop sign!" And, "Is that a cop?" I kind of wished it was a cop. Maybe they'd get pulled over and in trouble for having a girl with a pillowcase over her head in the car. I thought I recognized Zach's voice. And obviously Dallin's, but I wasn't sure who else was there. It could've just been the two of them. Eventually this case would be off my head so I tried to keep myself under control.

After at least ten minutes of obnoxious one-liners, the car slowed. I hadn't managed to keep myself under control at all. I could feel the sweat and tears streaked down my face. There was probably some snot too. But they weren't done. One last shout made my heart stand still. It was Dallin's voice. "Hey, look, your boyfriend is here, Autumn! I didn't know he like basketball."

And for the first time the entire ride, I heard Jeff. He laughed. He thought it was a joke. It wasn't a joke, but it was an exaggeration on Dallin's part. Dax was definitely not my boyfriend.

"Are you pointing at Dax Miller?" Jeff asked.

"Yes, you should ask Autumn about him. They got real tight while you were under." I wanted to punch Dallin. I understood that he might hate me for his various annoying reasons right now, but didn't he understand timing, that he was hurting his best friend?

The car pulled to a stop and I was helped out of it. I struggled until someone freed me and removed the pillowcase. All I could think about was getting out of there. I wanted out of there.

"Autumn," Jeff said, and I met his eyes. He was wheeling himself around the van we must've just emerged from. "Calm down. It's just us."

I looked around to see Lisa and Zach, Connor, Morgan and Avi, too. They were all staring at me like I was a little bit crazy. I wiped at my face, still trying to figure out where I could run to.

"You knew it was us, right?" Lisa asked.

"She saw me and heard us the entire time," Dallin said. "I don't know what she's freaking out about."

"Nothing. I'm freaking out about nothing. That's what happens sometimes when you have an anxiety disorder and someone shoves a bag over your head and ties you up. I have anxiety!" I yelled this at the top of my voice. "Does that make you happy, Dallin? To know that you just triggered an attack?"

As one, my group of friends seemed to step closer to me, closing the circle.

"I can't," I said. "I just need space. Just give me some space." I pushed between Lisa and Avi and ran across the parking lot all the way to the greenhouse, where I shut myself inside and tried to figure out how I was going to get home.

CHAPTER 45

• • • • • • •

I felt the burst of wind through the door before I realized someone had opened it. For the last fifteen minutes I had sat huddled on the dirty floor of the greenhouse analyzing my performance tonight. It was pretty epic. Me, looking crazed and wild, yelling about panic attacks, while my friends wondered how their practical joke had resulted in such a major overreaction. I knew I had been overreacting at the time, but it wasn't something I could stop. And now, outside of it, when my body had calmed down and my tears were dry, I knew it even more. I wondered who else had seen me in that parking lot, surrounded by my friends like I was some feral cat they were trying to tame. They'd said Dax was there. Had he already gone into the gym by that time? I didn't care. I wasn't going to think about Dax. Until now, when the door opened and for one heart-stopping moment, I thought it might be him.

But it wasn't. It was Jeff. He was standing, his wheelchair abandoned behind him. A single light outside the building reflected off the fog on the glass and created an eerie glow over the dead plants around me.

"Hey," he said, walking slowly. I wasn't sure if it was because he was still unsteady on his feet or if it was for my benefit.

I stood up and brushed off my pants. "Hi."

"You okay?"

"Getting there."

He came to a stop next to me and leaned up against a long table.

"So you have anxiety attacks?"

"Yes."

"Why didn't you tell us?"

"Because I didn't want you to treat me different."

He nodded back toward the door. "You wanted us to treat you the same?"

I laughed a little. "I thought I did. But I guess not."

"I'm sorry."

"It's not your fault," I said. "I should've told you. I should've told everybody."

He put his hand on my shoulder. "I've been looking for you for the last fifteen minutes. Lisa wanted to come too. She was worried about you." He met my eyes, his soft and questioning. "Should I have let her?"

"No. We need to talk." I couldn't put this off anymore.

"Is this about Dax Miller?"

"Dax is . . . was . . . a good friend. I had hoped for more. I care about him. But he's not into me like that."

"So I'm second choice?"

"No. Jeff, you know I care about you, but not like that."

He laughed, which surprised me. "Ouch. So I'm no choice at all."

His ever-present smile was on, and I couldn't tell if it was to hide his hurt or if this really wasn't affecting him at all.

"I'm sorry," I said.

"I want to throw a major tantrum right now because I really want you to like me."

"But?"

"But that would be ungrateful of me. You've given up a lot of time for me over the past several weeks. My mom told me how much you'd been by and how much you helped. So even though I wish you liked me as much as you like Dax, I'm going to be a big person, swallow my pride and hurt, and tell you to go be happy . . . after I kiss you."

"Tha—wait, what?"

"If you'll let me, of course. We've flirted around our feelings for months now and I just want to see if it would seal the deal for me at all. I'm an exceptional kisser."

"I . . ." Was he being serious? I couldn't tell with Jeff. We *had* flirted for months, and maybe it would help. Liking Jeff would make my life so much easier. "I don't want to lose you as a friend. Wouldn't that just make things weird?"

"What if I promise not to be weird after?"

More rules. And it seemed like none of them had stuck. I knew I didn't owe this to Jeff, but maybe I owed it to myself. So that I never looked back and wondered what would have happened if I had.

He closed his eyes and I moved forward to meet him, then stopped. This wasn't what I wanted. I was doing it again, trying to make someone else happy. We were so close that I had to put my finger on his lips to stop the kiss. "I can't," I whispered. "I don't want this."

He rested his forehead on mine instead. "It was worth a try."

I backed away.

His eyes went over my shoulder, locking on something

behind me. I looked as well but only saw the still-open door and his empty wheelchair.

"What is it?" I asked.

"It . . ." He shook his head. "Nothing. It was nothing."

"I'm sorry I didn't know what I wanted until now. And that I've been jerking you around for months," I said, remembering what Dallin had told me before.

"Jerking me around?" he asked. "You weren't. I think we were both testing our feelings. You just seemed to go the opposite way as me."

I stared at him in front of me, so tall and strong and steady. "I'm glad you're better, Jeff."

"Me too."

"Still friends?"

"Of course," he said. "You think our other friends would leave the basketball game early with us to get milk shakes?"

"I think our friends do anything you say."

"I thought so too, but you kind of proved that theory wrong tonight." He smiled at me. "Or I can take you home. Would you rather go home?"

I thought about that, analyzed how I felt. A weight seemed to be lifted off my shoulders and chest, and I felt better than I had in a while. "No, I want to go to Iceberg."

★ ★ ★

An hour later we were all sitting around a long table eating our shakes and fries at Iceberg. I tapped my cup on the table to get everyone's attention. "Sorry I didn't tell you all."

Lisa put her hand on my arm. "You should've. We love you no matter what." The rest of my friends called out saying various versions of that sentiment.

"Thank you." It was hard to remember what I'd been so scared of. Being treated differently? Lack of acceptance? I was the one who hadn't accepted myself for who I was. I was the one who needed to be comfortable in my own skin. I hoped I could do that moving forward.

Lisa cleared her throat from beside me and said under her breath, "Look who just walked in."

I did look. It was Dax. I was stuck in the middle of the table on the bench side, unable to get out. Not that I was anxious to.

Dax walked by where the nine of us were sitting and up to the register.

"I have a confession to make," Jeff said quietly from my other side.

"What?"

"He saw us earlier in the greenhouse."

"What?"

"When we almost kissed. He probably thought we did

kiss from that angle. I thought I was protecting you by not saying anything."

"Protecting me?"

"I've heard rumors about him."

"Jeff." An anger rose up my chest.

"I know. Don't be mad. I'm telling you now because I saw the way you looked at him when he walked in here. This is more than just a passing crush."

Dax had paid for something that he held in a brown paper bag and was now headed for the door. I was stuck, two people on my right, two on my left.

"I have your back," Jeff said, then he called out, "Dax!"

Dax turned and Jeff motioned him to come over. He did.

Jeff, unable to keep his jokester in check for long, said, as he threw his arm around my shoulder, "Were you looking at my girl?"

I elbowed him in the side and he laughed. I thought Dax would deny it, scoff at Jeff and leave, sensing he was the butt of some joke, but he stood his ground, met Jeff's stare head on. "Yes. I was."

That got the attention of everyone at the table, including me. But I wasn't feeling exceptionally charitable toward Dax considering our last interaction.

"Glad you're feeling better," Dax said to Jeff. Then to me, "Glad everything is back to normal."

I definitely didn't owe Dax an explanation, not after how he'd treated me. A couple of weeks ago, regardless of what Dax had done, I'd have been tempted to explain everything, make sure he still liked me.

Instead of responding to his statement I said, "You're still wearing your bracelet." I had taken mine off after the fight we had in the car.

His eyes went to my bare wrist. "It reminds me of a relationship I don't want to lose."

My heart skipped a beat. "But you've branded yourself unattached," I said. "Uncommitted."

He nodded his head to me, then waved to the rest of the table. "See you all later."

"Aren't you going to go after him?" Lisa asked as Dax walked out the door.

I looked at the other faces of my friends, the ones who didn't know my history with Dax. The ones whose looks only registered confusion. I wasn't sure I wanted to go after him. I knew my heart was racing. I knew I cared about him. But the thought of letting him in again scared me.

"If you don't, I might," Jeff said. "That was hot."

I laughed. "Let me out." I needed to at least hear what he had to say. I pushed Lisa, and Avi beside her. They didn't move fast enough, so I climbed over the top of the table.

"Seriously?" Dallin asked, having to move his shake and fries so they didn't end up in his lap.

"Shove it," I said, not caring for one second what he thought right now. Jeff laughed behind me.

It had taken me too long to get outside. The sidewalk was empty. I looked up and down the street out front, hoping there was a bus stop. I didn't see one. Dax was nowhere in sight. I whirled around and rushed to the end of the building, then peered around the corner. Dax was there, leaning against the brick wall.

My breath caught in my throat and I stopped short of joining him, lingering just far enough away to be out of reach. "Hi," I said.

"Hey. Thanks for coming out."

I nodded and rubbed at the goose bumps that had sprung onto my arms. He shrugged out of his jacket and held it out for me.

"That's okay. I'm good." I wasn't even sure how long I would be out here. I didn't need to be wrapped in his scent while trying to think clearly.

He didn't put his jacket back on, just clutched it in his grip. "I went to the game hoping to see you, but it wasn't good timing. I knew you and your friends normally come here after a game, so I thought I'd come because I needed to talk to you. I feel . . ." He looked up at me instead of at the ground where he'd been staring.

"I feel terrible for how I treated you the other day. I'm sorry. You didn't deserve that. I know you meant well. I want to say I acted that way because I was shocked to see my mom or that I was scared of how I was feeling about you, but there is no excuse for how I acted."

"Thank you." I wanted him to walk closer, to take the first step because I couldn't. He'd hurt me and I was the one with the wall up now.

"I shouldn't have kissed you."

"What?"

"You warned me about what would happen if I kissed you and I didn't listen."

I gave a breathy laugh.

He smiled. It was a sad smile, not what I'd grown used to, but it still managed to twist my heart. "No, that's a lie. I was attached before the kiss. Jeff really is a nice guy and one lucky SOB."

A laugh burst out of me and I covered my mouth.

Dax pushed himself off the wall and I knew he was leaving now that he'd said his piece. I thought about letting him because the thought of that day in the car still physically hurt.

But I couldn't. Even though I knew this might end in heartbreak, that he might make my life scary and complicated and unpredictable, I knew I couldn't let him walk away. Because I knew he'd also make my life happy and comforting and full. "Jeff and I aren't together."

He stopped, one foot out in front of him, his hands still wrapped around his jacket. "You're not?"

"Turns out I don't follow rules either."

"How so?"

"I became attached to someone I'd said I wouldn't too."

"I sure hope you mean me."

I nodded. He took the three big steps to reach me and picked me up in a hug. I could feel his heart beating against my chest, fast and hard.

I closed my eyes and buried my face in the space between his shoulder and neck.

A shiver went down my spine, and he pulled away and wrapped his jacket around my shoulders, then pulled me close again, his lips millimeters from mine.

"Are you sure you're ready for this?" I asked.

"What?"

"Commitment."

He smiled. "You make it easy."

CHAPTER 46

● ● ● ● ● ● ●

"You sure you want to go to this party? We don't have to," Dax said.

It was the next night, and Dax was in my room scrolling through pictures on my computer. He'd met my parents earlier. It went pretty well. It was more embarrassing than anything. My parents loved him. Fawned all over him, really. Mainly because of the whole rescuing-me-at-the-library scenario they had in their heads. And I wasn't going to correct them, because he really had helped me in the library. I couldn't imagine how much more panicked I would've been without him there.

My mom kept shaking his hand and saying, "It's so great to meet you. So great."

My dad said, "You two know each other from school, too?"

"Yes," I said. "We go to the same school. We didn't really know each other before the library, though."

"And now you're taking my daughter out?" my dad said with a smile. "The library brought you together." Then he looked up like he was reading something written across the air in front of him. "'Books, bringing people together.' That would make a good slogan for the library."

"I don't think you're the first to have thought of that one, Dad," I said.

He smiled. "I think my daughter is saying that I'm not as much of a genius as I think I am."

I patted his arm. "No, you're definitely as much of a genius as you think you are."

"Was that an insult?" he asked me, narrowing his eyes.

"I don't think so," I said.

He laughed.

"We're going to go to my room now while I finish getting ready."

"Can I get you anything?" my mom asked Dax. "Water, a snack . . . ?"

I thought she was going to finish that sentence with

the words *a hug* so I took Dax by the hand and led him away. He had been so quiet during the exchange that I was worried he was going to change his mind about wanting to be committed to someone if that commitment came with parents like mine.

"Sorry," I said.

"No, I'm sorry. I'm not really good with parents. I didn't know what to say. They were really nice. I'll get better."

I laughed and pulled him into a hug. "You're the cutest. And you did fine. I think you're already their favorite. You don't have to do much now."

"Cutest?"

I kissed him. "Yes, is that not an adjective you like?"

"I can live with it."

I smiled and pointed to my beanbag chair. "Sit. I need to finish getting ready."

Instead of sitting, Dax started walking around my room, looking at the pictures on my walls. Some were ones I'd taken, some were by photographers I admired. He stopped at my dresser to look at candid shots of my friends and me. I hadn't thought in the last twenty-four hours to look through those pictures and take down ones that might bother him. Like the one I'd stared at for months of Jeff and me, his arm slung over my shoulder, me looking at him instead of the camera.

I shook it off. It was too late now.

I grabbed my mascara and walked to my full-length mirror.

Dax nodded his head toward the pictures. "Did you take any of these?"

"No. Well, I mean, yes, probably some of them. But those are just ones from my phone or that friends texted me. My real ones are on my computer."

"Can I see them?"

"You want to see them?"

"Of course."

I grabbed my computer and powered it on. Then I pulled up my photo library and handed my laptop to him. He sat in the chair and began scrolling through it.

I watched him for a nervous moment, while I still held my open mascara, and that's when he looked up and asked the question. "Are you sure you want to go to this party? We don't have to."

"I actually feel good today. I think I'll be good."

"We could go on a hike instead. There's this gorgeous trail that's quiet and overlooks the valley. I think you'd like it."

That did sound amazing. "Yes."

"Yes?"

"Yes. Let's do that tomorrow."

He nodded hesitantly, then looked back at the

computer. "These are really good, Autumn. This one of the frozen web is amazing."

"You don't think I'll be good at the party?"

"No, it's not that."

That's when it hit me. "Oh! *You* don't want to go to this party."

He chuckled. "I'm sure you've noticed, I'm not great with . . . well . . . people."

I smiled, tossed my mascara back on the dresser, and sank to the floor next to him. "You're great with me."

He put aside the computer and pulled me up onto the beanbag chair next to him.

I ran my fingers through his hair. "We don't have to stay long. It's just the celebration for Jeff getting out of the hospital and, you know, being alive and stuff. I feel like it's important that I go. And I want you to go with me. Officially meet my friends."

He wrapped his arms around my waist and held me close. Maybe I didn't want to go to the party after all.

"I have something for you," he said.

"You do?"

He shifted and pulled something out of his pocket. It was a bright pink bracelet.

I lowered my brow. "Where did you get that? I threw mine away."

"I figured as much. I went by the library." He took my wrist and tied it there, then held up his own wrist.

The bracelet, which he'd always worn on his right hand, was now on his left, crossing the tattoo. He didn't say anything. He didn't have to. I leaned my forehead on his shoulder, a smile on my face.

It was loud and noisy and crowded, just like the last party Dallin had thrown. I reminded myself there was an empty laundry room available anytime I needed it. That seemed to settle down my fast-beating heart. Not to mention Dax's hand in mine. I led him through the crowd, introducing him to different people, including Jeff and Dallin, until I found Lisa.

She hip-checked me. "Hey, baby. You made it. And you brought your boy." She smiled at Dax. "Hi, I'm Lisa."

"Hi," Dax said.

"I've seen you around. Most recently last night at Iceberg where you were trying to win over my best friend."

Dax held up our linked hands. "I think I won."

She nodded. "You won the best heart in the world, so take care of it."

I looked at Lisa in surprise. She wasn't normally so sentimental.

She met my stare, then said, "Can I steal you to dance with me, or would you rather stay here where it's less crowded?"

"I would love to dance with you." I squeezed Dax's hand. "You good?"

"I'm fine."

Lisa dragged me to the middle of the crowd. "I didn't have a chance to talk to you last night at all."

"I know. I was kind of busy falling for a boy and stuff."

She laughed. "I'm glad you came tonight. I was worried after last night you'd feel . . . I don't know . . ."

"Stupid?"

"No, not stupid, but embarrassed or something. I was worried you wouldn't want to hang out with us. I'm sorry about the whole kidnapping thing."

I shook my head. "No, it's okay. I knew it was all supposed to be innocent and fun but I couldn't convince my body of that. My brain and body don't play well together sometimes."

"I'm sorry."

I shrugged. "It's life. Most of the time it's manageable. I still want to live, you know?"

"I know. I'm glad you came."

"Me too."

After the song was over she leaned close and said, "Should you rescue him?"

I glanced over my shoulder to see Dax surrounded by Jeff, Dallin, Zach, and Connor.

"I'll give him a minute and see how he does."

"He seems good for you," Lisa said. "More calm or stable or, I don't know—you two just fit."

"We do."

"It doesn't hurt that he's very easy on the eyes."

I laughed and looked over at the group of guys again. Jeff, Dallin, and the others were laughing and talking animatedly, occasionally punching or shoving each other. And Dax stood there, a small smile on his face, just listening, his body still. Then his eyes met mine and he said something and left them, heading my way

I squeezed Lisa's arm. "I'm going to dance with my boyfriend now."

She smiled. "I'm going to go flirt."

"Have fun."

Dax reached my side, took me by the hand, and led me up the stairs and down two halls without saying a word. I wasn't sure if Jeff or one of the other guys had said something or if something else was bothering him until he opened the door to the laundry room, led me inside, and closed it behind us.

"You okay?" I asked.

"Just thought we needed to visit our favorite room in this house."

I laughed and he pulled me into a hug.

"You want to dance?" I asked. The music was muted but still audible.

He swayed me back and forth much slower than the beat of the music.

"So now that you've committed to a girl, maybe you can go to class more, or even get a cat," I said.

I could feel his cheek, pressed against mine, turn up in a smile. "One step at a time, Autumn, one step at a time."

ACKNOWLEDGMENTS

To all of you out there who live with anxiety, depression, or other mental illnesses, you are seen. I know there are days where you feel like you've conquered a beast and days where you feel like it has conquered you. Thanks for being you and battling on.

This is my seventh book! Seventh?! How did that happen? I'll tell you how it happened, you readers. You inspire me to keep writing with your encouragement and love. You make me want to write more stories and explore new characters because you keep coming back for more. Thank you! Writing is my favorite, and I am so happy I can keep doing it.

I'd like to give a big thanks to Erika Hill at the Provo Library in Utah, who has hosted my friends and me for signings for the last several years. The Provo Library inspired this book. It is a gorgeous library. Thanks for the special tour when you found out I was writing *By Your Side* because it showed me that not only is the library gorgeous, it is also seriously cool (bell towers for the win). I did have to make some adjustments to the library for the purposes of the story, but overall I tried to stay true to the feel of the building.

As always, I'd like to thank my agent, Michelle

Wolfson. You have been there since the beginning, through all the ups and downs of this industry, and without you, I'd probably be lost by now. Or at least more lost. You are an awesome support and friend.

Thank you, Catherine Wallace, my editor. You are very good at making my vision better. Thanks for believing in my stories and making them come to life. And to the rest of my Harper team—Jennifer Klonsky, Stephanie Hoover, Elizabeth Ward, Tina Cameron, Bess Braswell, Jon Howard, Maya Packard, Michelle Taormina, Alison Klapthor, the Epic Reads girls, and others I'm sure I'm missing—thank you!

My husband, Jared, has become the first reader of my stories, and he is awesome at giving me the confidence I need before I send it to the people who have to tear it apart so I can make it better. Not only does he read my stories, he supports me in everything I do. In fact, I'm writing this thank-ology during the Rio Summer Olympics and I told him I wanted to take up rowing. He said: "We'd better move to Michigan, then." (For the record, I probably won't take up rowing.) I love you, Jared.

Isn't it weird how I keep switching back and forth between first person and second person. Aren't you glad I'm better at writing books than I am at writing acknowledgments? Unless you hate my books. Then it's probably a toss-up for you.

This paragraph will also be about my family. My kids are awesome. I know other people think their kids are the best, but I pretty much won the kid lottery (I should've saved that line for my next book, which is about winning the lottery. Acknowledgments Spoiler Alert, my next book's acknowledgments section will have the "kid lottery" line again). Hannah, Autumn, Abby, and Donavan, thank you for always supporting me and for being pretty laid-back kids who know how to make me laugh. I love you all so much.

I also have some amazing writer friends who are always around to help me iron out a story or brainstorm ideas or stay up until three a.m. at writers' conferences making me laugh so hard I cry. So much love to: Candice Kennington, Jenn Johansson, Renee Collins, Natalie Whipple, Michelle Argyle, Sara Raasch, Bree Despain, Jeff Savage, Tyler Jolley, Charlie Pulsipher, Michael Bacera. I shouldn't have started naming names. Now I'm going to miss someone awesome and feel terrible.

That said, I'm going to name more names. I mean, that's kind of what this section is about. On to nonwriter friends who I love and who keep me grounded: Stephanie Ryan, Rachel Whiting, Elizabeth Minnick, Claudia Wadsworth, Misti Hamel, Brittney Swift, Mandy Hillman, Emily Freeman, and Jamie Lawrence.

Last, but not least, my amazing extended family. Are you ready for another long list of names of people I love so much? Here it comes: Chris DeWoody, Heather Garza, Jared DeWoody, Spencer DeWoody, Stephanie Ryan, Dave Garza, Rachel DeWoody, Zita Konik, Kevin Ryan, Vance West, Karen West, Eric West, Michelle West, Sharlynn West, Rachel Braithwaite, Brian Braithwaite, Angie Stettler, Jim Stettler, Emily Hill, Rick Hill, and the twenty-five children that exist among all these people.

BY YOUR SIDE

Books by Kasie West

Pivot Point
Split Second

The Distance Between Us
On the Fence
The Fill-In Boyfriend
P.S. I Like You

ALSO BY KASIE WEST

Find love where you least expect it!